Without God

I Am. Nothing.

Goulds, Florida Forever!

Some Men Wear Panties

Dapharoah69

The King of Erotica

£a®~®¥

╬.Ķ.Φ.Є. Publications

PUBLISHED BY LARRY WILSON, JR.

GOULDS, FLORIDA

ISBN 978-0-578-04517-7 90000

9 780578 045177

PHOTOS BY JOHN WILSON AND LARRY WILSON, JR.

LIBRARY OF CONGRESS CATALOGING-IN-PUBLICATION DATA HAS BEEN APPLIED FOR.

PAPERBACK VERSION PUBLISHED BY URBAN MOON

JL KING

MY VERSION HARD COVER (SOME MEN WEAR PANTIES)

PUBLISHED BY LARRY WILSON, JR.

TKOE PUBLICATIONS

Some Men Wear Panties

Who said fantasies and fetishes are bound to just the Woman?
Well…you are in for a rude awakening!
The King of Erotica Style.
If you don't know by now.
I DON'T FOLLOW RULES!

Ac.know.ledge.ments

I want to sincerely apologize to anyone who ordered this book back in March 2009, when I thought it was coming out around that time. Many lies have been told to me with the creation of this book. Many promises were made that blew up in my face while the person who was supposed to publish this book traveled the country, doing plays, promoting his own books, doing his own book tour while I sat like a dumb ass with my life on hold twiddling my thumbs. From now on I'm *not* doing *any* projects for anybody unless they are my own with a contract and for a fee.

I own everything with my name on it. I am my own CEO and my manager is GOD. Every decision I make with my work, whether good or bad, aids the progress of my work and my own personal development. This book is different for me. And at first I didn't want to write it. With each project I channel a different part of me, something that is real, raw and uncensored. My books are testaments of growth, progress and stamina.

When bestselling author J.L. King pitched the idea to me I was excited to write this book. I wrote this in two days and was done with it. The original version was supposed to be published by Urban Moon Publications. But after waiting for almost a year, I decided to do it on my own. But now I here it's available at Outwrite Bookstore in Atlanta. Cool.

I have yet to sign a contract though. I'll just sit back and wait.

When Plan A presents itself I always have a Plan B because I can't just sit back and let people do things for me. That's not how I operate. I take control of my own destiny. I MAKE things happen for myself. As always I write things from the heart and I do it bluntly.

I don't care what anyone has to say about my work. Just read it and get something from it and move on to another book. All thanks and the glory go to GOD before I EVER thank mortal man.

Without GOD nothing would be possible. I want to thank Kevin McNeir for his brilliant editing. He didn't get editing credits in the paperback version, which was put together without my say, so I give him credit in the hard cover version. I want to thank Fran Briggs, my publicist and very dear friend. She listened to me during a very trying time.

I want to thank Chenelle Covin for creating the website. I want to thank John Wilson for being there with me during the hardships. I want to thank Jimmy Grant for showing me how to let go some bitterness when it came to my past. I want to thank Kevin R. Palmer, B.A., M.I.B. my case manager.

You are a very beautiful man inside and out and your passion for helping others and putting yourself on the back burner is a blessing from God. For Meredyeth T. Lighthouse, M.A., Ed. S. for all the love, support and the attention you give me. I thank God for all of you.

For my Face Book Family. You all have been there and offered some good advice. And I appreciate each and every one of you. For **E. Lynn Harris.**

Thanks for the love, the advice and for allowing me to be featured in your Literary Café. I knew then that I had arrived and was here to stay. For Attica Lundy, my God sister. I love you and thanks for taking care of me for five weeks when I visited Atlanta.

I promote HIV Awareness in all my work now. I have also become a spokesperson for it. I am dedicating my time to saving lives, speaking about it at conferences and trying to show the troubled youth a better way. I love the gift that GOD has bestowed on me. I appreciate every book I've written.

I represent Goulds to the fullest.

That's my hometown and I love making it look good. For whoever has a dream. Work for it, it'll happen. Don't wait for others to do it for you. Do it for yourself.

Love always,

Dapharoah69

The Panty Drawer:

Grandma's Panties
Luscious
The Atomic Bomb
The Locked Room
Closed Until Further Notice
The Basketball Court
The Salon
What Goes Around
Obese Booty Call
Assembly Line
The Lesbian
Choke
The Dressing Room

Grandma's panties…

My name is Brandisha Sinclair and good pussy runs in the family. When I was growing up my Grandma Quanisha, a sweet, homely woman was my idol. I looked up to her. I used to model myself after her. My love for God and my appreciation for all selfless things stemmed from her love. I used to love her sweet potato pies she made from scratch. She always made my very own pie and she didn't let anybody touch it. I remember sitting on the dining table watching her mix the ingredients. She always took her time. She never needed measuring cups. She knew just how much spice or sugar to add. She would always kiss my lips and tell me I was beautiful. I would blush with glee and never question her judgment.

A strikingly gorgeous woman, Grandma always wore the sexiest panties known to man. She spent more on her underwear than she spent on make-up and other bare necessities. She had a quiet sex appeal about her that wasn't rushed, coerced or forced. She had a bubbling personality and she never let anybody steal her thunder. She knew who she was as a woman and I always modeled myself after that. She wasn't an avid drinker, but three days a week she drank red wine and I'm not talking about that cheap shit.

She worked out, doing cardio on Tuesdays and Thursdays to keep herself in shape. She was so buff people thought she was my mother and they gawked at her when she told them I was her only granddaughter. When I was seven- years-old I started jogging with her. That kept me in shape. She didn't smoke and she ate a lot of fruits.

As far as relationships go, Grandma never really had a steady boyfriend. She was the type who liked to tell her men what to do and if they didn't listen then she hit the road and never came back. Men were tearing down the door trying to own and possess her. They used to bring her roses and daisies and lilies and chocolates and she would always return the gifts and say one thing that baffled me as a child: "I don't know your intentions for buying me these things. I make my own money. I don't need your dangling carrots!"

I learned then that men always wanted to own and possess the things they didn't understand or things they couldn't fuck or control.

As a little nappy-headed girl, I needed to see strong women -- watching how they handled financial hardships and studying how they dealt with everyday people with situations a child must experience. It was one thing to watch Aretha Franklin and Josephine Baker open doors for female entertainers, but it's another to see people you knew doing that as well. Grandma was comfortable in her own skin and Mama was always jealous of that.

In comparison to my Mother, Grandma had her shit together. Mama was a scary bitch who buckled in battle, didn't talk much and was afraid of her own shadow. She was a selfish woman. Everything that she did had to benefit her in some way. If she didn't get what she wanted then the hell with everybody.

On Sunday evenings, Grandma used to cook big dinners and sing Aretha Franklin songs, snapping her fingers. She wore the same jet-black wig. It made her eyes seem exotic. She looked so youthful and I got a thrill out of witnessing it. I can remember one day, when Grandma was in the shower, I crept into her room and put the wig on my head. Smiling, I turned to face myself in the mirror. Something seemed off. I was giggling, covering my mouth. I looked just like her. I opened her panty drawer and I rummaged through her panties. There were red ones, black ones and satin ones. Wow, Grandma.

I heard her humming from the shower. My hand bumped into a hard object and I pulled it out. It was a toy of sorts. It looked like the same thing between Daddy's legs. I wondered what it was for. Grandma told me there was no such thing as a stupid question. So I walked towards the bathroom door. I knocked, then opened it. Steam hit me in the face. Smelled tart in there. I was starting to perspire.

"Grandma!"

She opened the shower curtain with foamy soap all over her body and face.

"Yes, Baby?"

I held up the toy. "What's this?"

Alarmed, I never saw a woman run so fast. The color leaving her face, she snatched the toy from me and slapped me across the head with it. "Why did you go into my shit?" I started to cry. She slapped me with it again.

"Whack!"

"Answer me, little girl! WHY DID YOU GO IN MY SHIT?"

"I just wanted to be like you, Grandma!"

I was crushed. She'd never raised her hand to me and now that she raised the toy to my head things seemed instantly different.

"GET OUT OF HERE! AND PUT THE TOY BACK, GODDAMN IT!"

She gave it to me. Devastated, I replaced the toy, never to go through her shit again.

She used to perform for me in her panties and bra. She would imitate Eartha Kitt, Fred Astaire and Ginger Rogers. It took me a while to forgive her for slapping me with a plastic dick. I would never forget that for as long as I live. She would grab the hair brush and it became her microphone. She could have been a star if she wanted to be. But the only thing I didn't approve of was that she would wear them for a week straight and then wash them. I thought that was nasty but I was a little girl. I couldn't sass my Grandmother. She was a hard-working woman. She worked at a job I hated with a passion but it brought her money and kept a roof over her head.

Grandma once told me when I was eleven that she loved her pussy. She told me that I was too young to understand but pussy made the world go round.

She said pussy birthed life. Without pussy dick didn't have a natural habitat? I was confused about it. I asked her what she meant and she said, "Grab your pussy…like a man grabs his crotch."

Standing in the bathroom, I did. I didn't feel any different.

"Say, "This is my pussy! I will use it how I see fit!"'

"This is my pussy I will use it how I see fit."

"If a man doesn't respect me than he doesn't get the pleasure of my warmth."

I repeated the words. And each time I did, I felt empowered.

Now I loved my pussy. Sometimes I verbally said the word (PUSSY) and it made me wet. I was a cute bitch. I wore Gucci, Louis Vuitton and Prada because my Daddy, with his sick ass, always dressed for success and it rubbed off on me like a good dick against my clit. If it wasn't name brand then don't name shit.

I loved having the best. I loved *being* the best. When I joined the Air Force eight years ago, my taste in global things was born. I didn't have kids and I didn't *want* kids. I hated when some women told me I wasn't a complete woman if I didn't experience child birth. Um, correct me if I am wrong but when they had children at the age of fourteen and sixteen, they weren't "complete, whole women" either. So hearing that phrase contradicted the entire conversation. Just because you're stuck with children and a man who dogged you didn't mean that had to be my reality. I didn't have many women friends because they were messy bitches who wanted to take everything you owned. I had more male friends than anything.

The Tree of Life, my Fallopian tubes, the Tree God told Eve and Adam to never eat from, because it was the Tree that bared fruit, would forever be naked to the human eye. I thought about that while the Pastor of my church tried to convince the congregation that an "apple" was the forbidden fruit. No, Sir. I already didn't want to congregate with these phony people but sometimes it was nice to show up and show out. I shifted on the pew, my short dress inching up my thighs. My hair was un-be-weavable, my heels were long and edgy and my chandelier earrings sparkled with abandon. My long, slender legs seemed to grow from the core of the earth. I fanned myself, sweat racing down the split between my honey jugs.

Uneasy, I watched him pace back and forth, screaming into the microphone more than eloquently speaking, I had my own thoughts. The Serpent fucked Eve and when her eyes were opened from that intense orgasm, she gave Adam an orgasm and everything made sense and they covered up because they discovered they were naked. I stood up and said this and everyone was quiet. He challenged me and I challenged him.

"Let's keep it real, Pastor."

"Let's, pretty lady. I am open to discussion."

I gave a smile. "Sure."

He took a handkerchief from his upper jacket pocket and wiped sweat from his face. Maybe if he laid off the buffet at the Golden Coral his fat ass would have more stamina.

"Before we start...I have a degree in theology from UCLA. I have been a minister for thirty-two years. I have attended Bible Bowls, dined with some of the best Prime ministers and I know my craft."

"Amen!" several people boasted.

"Hallelujah, Amen!" another woman chanted and I rolled my eyes. This was the *same* woman who ate my pussy and sucked her husband's dick at the same time last week because her husband wouldn't eat hers. *So be it, huh, bitch?*

"Let's talk about this, Pastor. I challenge you. This is the House of God, made up of 3 percent realism, 45 percent whorism and 52 percent freakism."

Random people started ducking in the pews.

"The Garden of Eden was Eve's bushy vagina. God told Adam and Eve they could eat fruit from any tree in the garden but do not eat the *forbidden* fruit from the Tree of Life, the Tree that *bares* fruit. That's a contradiction. All the trees had fruit but *why* couldn't they eat fruit from the tree that *bared* fruit? Hmm. Because the tree he was referring to was her womb. Think of the shape of the fallopian tubes. The ovaries or ovum, if you will, are located on either end, right Pastor?"

"Amen!"

The church was in an uproar.

"Hallelujah! She speaks the truth!"

"Oh my God! I never thought about it like that!"

"Speak Sister!"

"The fallopian tubes *bare* fruit *doesn't it,* Mr. UCLA, Mr. Theology, in the form of seeds. When you dined with Prime ministers, did you know that? Um, no. A man's sperm fertilizes the seeds and life is created. The male penis has a urinary track that leads to the garden in Eve's womb. Sex is forbidden before marriage, is it not? So that would be the forbidden fruit, right Pastor? Correct me if I'm wrong. The Bible says for man and woman to multiply and be *fruitful.* Do you get my drift? So when the Serpent opened Eve's eyes she took her satisfied vagina to Adam and took his virginity, laying it on him and opening his eyes and he exploded in her and his eyes were wide, they were open and life was born. But let's be real…the Serpent exploded in her as well, so who did Eve really have the baby from? Adam? Or the Serpent. Thus evil vs. good was born, giving us complications out of this world…"

"I can't believe you would say that in the House…"

"…Stay tuned for the next episode of Maury Povich," I interrupted.

I didn't want to hear that sappy shit.

"*Pastor,* you are *not* the father!"

Everyone stood up, clapping and whistling and crying and screaming HALLELUJAH GOD!

My mission was done. Now all eyes were open. I grabbed my purse and walked towards the Exit door. My duty was done for the day. I hated when Pastors preached lies. Keep it real with the people. An apple tree isn't the goddamn Tree of Life and Knowledge. When I ate an apple, I didn't suddenly know Chinese arithmetic. When I ate an apple I didn't suddenly become a chemist. When I ate an apple I didn't suddenly become the best dick sucker in the world. If *that's* the case I ate an entire bag (BAGS) of apples in college and I barely passed with a goddamn C! When I ate an apple it kept the doctor away and my panties around my ankles when the red peelings pushed my ass to the toilet.

All an apple did was regulate your digestive system.

Eden wasn't destroyed over a fucking apple. Eve's pussy failed her. And it cost her and Adam dearly.

And ran me $500 a year in feminine products because God punished me by making my pussy bleed once a month.

In my living room were headless busts from Rome, a few Egyptian pieces from Alexandria, Egypt…fancy dolls above the mantel of the fireplace. No, I didn't actually go to those places to buy those things. That's the power of EBay and Amazon.com. Everything you want was a click-of-the-mouse away. My small, two-bedroom, one-bath home was a reflection of me because growing up I had less-than-humble beginnings. I come from a long line of entrepreneurs. My Mama sold pussy like it was ice cream cake, Daddy pimped everyone from his own mother (Grandma Quanisha) to my mother. I never condoned or understood why he defiled his women but that was Daddy—not all there.

I remember when I was six-years-old, after she cooked us breakfast, Mama looked at me and said, "If it's not about money then baby it don't make sense." And I vowed to live differently when I was older. I knew then I wasn't going to have men in and out of my door.

It didn't take much to make me happy. I did know that one day I would care for my Grandmother. My Dad's Mom didn't want to sell her body but when she got the money she nearly justified it with excuses. She may have been a strong woman, the one I admired, but even the strong had weaknesses.

I knew I was a head strong bitch when my father tried to pimp me when I turned eighteen. At the time my pussy hadn't been popped and I was saving it for a special guy. Daddy sold me a pipe dream. He claimed times were hard, that Mama's pussy was washed up like wet dope and that I had enough spark to set California forests on fire and destroy some homes in the process making that money.

I remember staring at him in disbelief. I had just been sworn into the military and I was looking forward to seeing the world, leaving all the baggage of hate, rejection and fear behind to clutter the closets with Daddy's bullshit. I was looking cute, with my high heels, dangling diamond-drop earrings and plaid skirt with a rose-colored blouse.

"Are you serious, Daddy?" I asked, trying to be respectable. My perfume was wearing off and I needed to find my purse because it seemed to be missing.

He smiled, looking boyishly handsome in a beige suit with a cream feather in his fedora. He was rubbing his crotch, without making it obvious.

"Yes, darling. We could use it."

He never called me 'darling'. What are you up to, Daddy? It was very easy to fall for his lies. He was cunningly good. He could talk Satan and Jesus into being best friends if he wanted to. Daddy's lips have made women all over America have orgasms and empty purses. He even pimped himself. He didn't have a dick. His nuts and cock were joint ventures that merged into the NASDAQ. He bedded so many women they were still fighting each other to own his penis and for some strange reason he would never divorce Mom.

I glanced at his wedding photo. In it he hugged Mama possessively. Rumor had it he put Mama's pussy to work on the honeymoon when half the men booked in the hotel paid to beat the pussy up. Mama made $350 from the

$4,500 made and she had to bathe in Epsom salt-clad water to heal the aching muscles. She couldn't talk to men alone. Daddy had to be present. Even when she sold her pussy Daddy was the supervisor on the clock. He was there, coaching her and telling her what to do. If she didn't suck a dick right he whipped her ass with his cane in front of the client.

I shook the thoughts away.

"Baby, are you hearing me…"

"Hearing what, Daddy?"

"We could use the money."

"We could *use* it?"

He grinned, sipping his Hennessy. "Yes."

"Have you lost your mind?"

"No, baby. I'm trying to invest in your future."

My brows rose. "By selling my pussy?"

"No. By *investing* in your pussy, ass, hands and lips. You let your boyfriend fuck you for free anyway!"

"I haven't had sex yet, Daddy. I'm still a virgin."

"That's even better. Sister Mary Pussy is the best. Why have a Wal-Mart pussy, giving it up to a broke niggah in the future when you can build your brand into Wall Street material? My dick is pure Grade A beef. I select pussy like I select a meat plan. You want to select the best one on the board."

"I resent that shit, Daddy!" I was insulted.

"Sometimes you can talk a man out of his wallet without having to do anything."

"You're sick, Daddy! Where is your heart?"

"Soaking in your Mama's panties."

I stood up from the table, sighing. I didn't have time for this.

"No, Daddy. I am going to see the world."

He was getting upset. He was the ruler of the kingdom and what he said went but that shit only worked when I was a little girl. I was grown, got my high school diploma and I didn't have time for men and their egotistical plights.

"Baby. Come here."

I walked over to him. Despite the sickness in his brain I loved the man. He was my father and in my own way I thanked God I knew my dad. He had a fun, loving side but when he dropped in that happiness too deeply he snapped and became another person and I never understood why.

He embraced me. I wrapped my arms around him. He smelled good.

"Baby, your mama and I need your services."

"Dad, I leave for the Air Force soon."

"So your obligation is to Uncle Sam?"

"And to myself."

He pulled away from me, rubbing my face. He had soft eyes. I had his eyes.

"Please…"

"No, Daddy."

"Is that your final answer, Sweetheart?" His voice was seductive.

Tears fell from my eyes. "Yes."

The demon surfaced. Stomping on my foot, he slapped me so hard I flipped in the air and fell on my face. He leaned down and snatched my hair, pulling me to his face. He gave a chilling smile, making my skin crawl.

"You will do what the fuck I say, bitch!" he said, while releasing my hair. He towered over me and lit a cigarette. I realized I had never known this kind of pain. He had never raised his hand to me.

Then pulling on the cigarette, he dumped ashes on me, putting a Gucci-clad foot on my back.

"This is what you're going to do. You are going to go in my bedroom and get the list on my dresser. On it are names of men who pay handsomely for quality pussy. I have a menu of prices in the top drawer of my armoire. Are you listening, bitch? I love money and money makes my dick hard. Bring me what I ask for and I will make some calls. When you meet these men professionalism is a must. Fix them some coffee, never look in their eyes when you speak and if you offer anything for free, even your conversation, I will fuck you myself and beat your ass bitch."

Keeping the cigarette in his mouth, he leaned down and pulled me to my feet, slapping me again. He took off his Gucci shoe and spanked my ass, holding my arm.

I was trying to fight him back but he was a bull, while I was a poodle. I was no match for him. He snatched me by the hair and pulled me to his face.

"Get to work bitch. You shit and piss in my home for free. Time to pay Daddy."

I was head strong. I get that from him. I gritted my teeth.

"Like hell I will. I am a Queen…"

He spat in my face. I was disgusted.

"You are a pretty whore."

He used his finger to wipe his spit in my face. I was about to puke.

"Your Mama spat on my dick the night I made you. She dressed in heels and a wig and was my dirty bitch. I didn't want a daughter or a son. But God gave me you when I needed an investment for the future. You see I knew your mother's pussy would be used and washed up by the time she reached a certain age. So investing in you, taking care of you, helping you with school work and giving you the best gave you a no nonsense, high maintenance attitude."

"Daddy."

"When you're on the clock it's 'Fancy Mancy,' not 'Daddy.'"

He kissed my lips. I shuddered in my heels.

"Before you go…know this. One day your pussy will be washed up…and I had to take precautions so your mother is pregnant with twin girls right now…You see how life imitates art? Pimping is pimping and I will not let my wife, or daughter, destroy the pimping game."

He put his foot on my ass and pushed me on the floor. I fell on my knees, and it hurt badly.

"Go do what I told you."

I ran to the front door and opened it. I had never sprinted so fast in my life. I didn't look back, I didn't want to look back…I would turn to salt. I was devastated and I felt alone. I ran and I ran…heading for the recruiter's office.

Air Force, here I come.

That was eight years ago. My life has changed for the better since then. My parents still live in Compton and I live on the other side of the world, in Savannah, Georgia. My grandmother lives with me and her life has prospered since I freed her from prostitution. She met an older man who treated her with respect and they were actually thinking of moving in together but I wasn't ready for her to be on her own. I had to protect her.

I was a staff sergeant when I got out of the Armed Forces. I used the G.I. Bill to elevate myself. I used my housing voucher to get a home. I never contacted my family again. I missed them, yes, but the things Daddy did to me were despicable.

I had good pussy. I played with my pussy every single day. I loved having orgasms. Some people liked to draw, other loved smoking pot…I loved playing in my garden. I loved the way my pussy looked.

I didn't classify it by the grade. Grade A, B and C were for little girls with report cards and progress reports and I was 32-years-old with good sushi and if you didn't like it you could suck my clit, pretend it's battered cat fish and *voila*, be done with it. But that's not why I chose to write this freaky account. I'm a whore of my man's subconscious. Daniel Boone Simmons knew I lived in his soul because when he woke up at 3 a.m., stroking his dick…the bitch in him, me of course, took his fingers and played with his asshole while he squirmed all over those damn sheets with my girlfriend's dried cum all over them. He loved the smell.

I was a little shy. I tapped into his fingertips and made him type this freaky shit you read now. Case in point: I had good pussy. Yes. When my man sucked the sliced peach he spat watermelon seeds. Since good pussy was passed down through generations of Sinclair's, I would make him suck my titties while I wore my Mama's bra. I tried to keep it cool but I did have a dilemma. It was about my man (go figure) and he got on my nerves.

He loved playing basketball with the fellahs and all those dicks swinging beneath the gym shorts turned me on. My pussy was wet just sitting on the bleachers with my friends watching my man jump, bend over, flag his arms and slap asses. I loved the way he patted the boys' asses. He seemed so absent-minded when he did so. But this was the thing. His dick was stinking. Oh my God. Wash your fucking dick. I thought he would get the point when I rubbed Ultra Brite toothpaste on his dick a month ago. Burned his ass. He got an attitude and didn't talk to me for a week. He told me I wasn't getting any dick. When I pulled my dildo from the nightstand he got the point. Niggah, I kept dick on stand by. I had a Passenger 57 pussy.

Then to make matters worse he started playing football and basketball in the evenings and came to my home, took off his shorts, his wife-beater soaked with sweat and he would shove his dick in my mouth, grinding against my tongue.

The shit pissed me off but I really couldn't protest because I wasn't working and he paid my rent and car note so what could I do?

He loved sniffing my panties but what I didn't tell him was that I stole my Grandma's panties before she did the laundry.

Those panties with a week worth of pussy juice were my revenge card.

I got them when they were soaked and drenched with her vaginal secretions and I would put them on, which were three sizes too small and it made my ass look plumper than it was. The lace rode my asshole like thongs and he would suck my clit through the lace, tasting three generations of pussy and that was the catch. I never told him the secret behind those sweet-tasting panties. I was a freak like that. I figured if he could eat my pussy then he could suck my clit through my Grandma's drenched panties, and she had a faucet in her vaginal walls that flowed worse than Indonesian rainfalls.

So the next time your man wants you to suck a funky dick, put on your Grandma's panties and get him before he gets you.

Thanks, Grandma.

Luscious

When the New Year started I told myself I would make affirmations I could live up to because last year I hadn't lived up to one single expectation I'd set for myself. And that's me. Always doing something I wasn't supposed to. We all had our days and we all had our nights but lately my nights seemed like muggy days and my cool days seemed like frustrated evenings with a touch of aggravation setting me off at any given moment. A few affirmations I made this year went as follows: I will get to work on time. I will treat my friends with respect. I will treat my best friend like royalty. I will love my girlfriend. I will. Love. My. Girlfriend. I WILL LOVE MY GIRL FRIEND. Hmm, maybe I shouldn't have made that one. Reason being was simple. Um, yes, I'm bisexual. *So what!* It's *my* goddamn life. I will do what I want to. In fact, I thought about climbing out of the window of my girl's house now. I always did, to go see a different niggah. I didn't do it a lot, though. Probably twice a month. Why didn't I go through the door? She got a new alarm put on it and when you opened the door it made that soul-lacerating buzzing sound that made me jump. It'd wake my Charles up from the dead and I didn't know the code to the alarm to cut it off. She went behind my back and had the codes changed because she claimed that she felt vulnerable when I used to turn it off.

"I got it in place so I know when somebody is opening my door."

"But I hate it, Boo."

"I know you do. But I like it. I have to be aware these days. Don't need anybody creeping up in here while we're sleeping…"

I thought about my sex romps with the fellahs being compromised.

"Nobody is going to come in here, Boo."

She hugged me and put her hands in my pants. My dick took a while to get hard. She didn't turn me on as much as she used to. Was it because I lusted after the fellahs? Maybe. Maybe not. I looked in her eyes and saw the love she had for me. And she always did this. Tried to give me some Shut Up, It's My Way Pussy to get me to go along with her request. And for the most part, since women were too emotional, I went along with it.

Now I lay in bed, wide awake. The clock tells me it's pouring into the wee hours of the morning. Her arm is over her face and she's snoring. She always slept like a brick. I could slide my dick in that pussy and she'd still be snoring.

I'm too slick with my shit. Plus Karma was on my side. I will never get caught up. I shouldn't creep out of windows, a bit childish if you asked me. But a niggah called me I hadn't fucked in ages and I wanted him. I looked at the side of her face, stroking her cheek. I thought about him instead of her. I knew I was wrong but damn, he used to give me the best orgasms of my life. She used to tell me that she took our sexcapades as something utterly sweet. That she allowed our sexual union to strengthen our relationship. Didn't she understand that I said whatever I had to say (in the beginning) just to fuck her? I just didn't imagine that I would develop feelings for her air-headed ass.

Knowing full damn well I was wrong for creeping, I slowly slid out of bed and cautiously walked across the room to the armoire. I opened it. It creaked a tad. She stirred and I held my breath. Watching. Observing. Good. She's still sleeping. She turned over and her ass was tooted in the air, her lips flapping like a horse.

I took out a pair of black sweat pants. I took off my boxers and kicked them under the dresser. I put on the sweats and then a long sleeved black shirt, a black hat and black socks. I closed the doors of the armoire and went to the closet and put on some all-black Jordans.

I looked at her, telling myself that I shouldn't cheat on her. But she was always nagging. Always doing things that pissed me off. Always going against what I asked for. Never cooked on time. Always bought shit outside of our budget. Stepped on my manhood. Thinking about it all upset me and I just had to act on it. There's no way she could keep getting away with treating me like I was her brother instead of her lover.

I walked down the stairs and looked at the alarm box. What was the code? I went snooping through her bills and letters on the dining table. Nothing. I then thought about the password to her cell phone. It was her birthday. I walked back to the alarm box and typed in her birthday and hit "Enter" and the door chime turned off. YES! Bingo!

I tiptoed out of the front door and was careful when I closed it. I left it unlocked. She'd be safe for the time being. I speed walked to my car, trying my best to will my nervousness back to where it came from. My hands shook as I fumbled in my pockets for the keys. I was looking round, surveying. Making sure no one saw me. I finally found my keys and they dangled noisily as I unlocked my ride. I didn't have an alarm on it nor did I want one. If someone stole my car they'd be doing me a huge favor. I could then call my insurance company and get another one.

I got in the driver's seat and put the car in reverse. I got out and pushed it back, the crickets chirping. When I got it in the road I turned it on, got inside and hot-trotted to his house, which was a couple of blocks away. He told me he owned his home and I was happy that he did because my money was funny and I didn't have enough to spot a hotel room.

I wondered exactly how long he had lived in my neighborhood because I hadn't seen him until a few days ago and it was like old times when we locked eyes. Every thing I thought I would never feel again came flooding back like I was Moses crossing the Red Sea and I couldn't keep it together. I wound up fucking him in the stall at Wal-Mart as an end result.

When I got to the impoverished home he opened the garage and I parked next to a SUV. Looking at him brought back so much. I am not giving my name or description. That's not important. What's important was the nut bubbling in my testicles, which wanted to be all over his handsome face.

With lust in his eyes, he opened my car door looking like a young Shemar Moore. He gives me some tongue and I am rubbing on his big ass. It was plump and soft. Just the way I remembered it. I had a quick flash of the red thongs he used to wear for me. He hated wearing anything on the feminine side but he had done it just to make me happy. Coyly, he unbuttons his shirt and takes it off and the soft glow of the garage lights bring out the beauty of his eyes. He pushes a control in his hand and the garage door closed with a noisy thud.

Gently, he pushes me on my car seat and gets on top of me. I felt so good. I had to make it quick. I looked at my watch. I really had to get a move on. Hit this booty hole and get home before my girl wakes up.

I hated to treat him like a whore but any man sucking my dick in the wee hours of the morning either had a habit or a problem. Either way it wasn't my problem. Looking as sexy as he wanted to be, he unbuttons my pants and pulls out my dick. He doesn't waste anytime. He started to lick on it with a fire I'd never seen before. Like he hadn't had dick in ages. Like he was hungry for it. Famished without it. Like a seasoned professional, he takes it to the tonsils in ways my girl wish she could. He slobbers all over it as I try to forget that I proposed to my girl a few weeks ago. We were set to marry and her cousin was supposed to be coming to town to be in the wedding and to help plan it. Some dude named Elroy Joseph who I had talked to on the phone but had never met.

This niggah still sucked a mean dick. Nothing had changed about it. I gave him time to enjoy the incredible inches. But now I wanted something more. I wanted to feel his tight asshole on my stick. I really needed a shot of ass so I slapped his booty and told him to let me out the car. Like a little bitch he turned around and pulled his pants down. He knew what I wanted.

I got on my knees and admired his gorgeous ass. I spread his cheeks and used my index fingers to make that hole say "*Aaaah*." I started to feast, slowly munching in his chocolate, my mustache tickling the hairs on his ass. Booty cheeks were on either side of my tongue. He moaned and I slapped his booty again. Smack. Smack. I stood up and slid in him. Fuck the rubber.

This one time wouldn't hurt.

I called him, "Luscious."

Ж

When I first met him at the mall he told me his name was George Samuels. I fell in love with him in nearly a day, but we had double lives so that was that.

I rummaged around in the ass, making him squirm. He could barely take it but I didn't care. I pulled out, slapping his ass cheeks with my dick. He gyrated that booty, loving it. I spread the cheeks and spit on that hole, tasting him. He died.

He told me he wanted to come so I let him sit on my seat and beat off while I pushed his legs back and ate him out like he was my girl. He loved it. When he had to come a few minutes later it squirted on his chest and I licked it up, swallowing him on impulse. I wanted some more ass so I went up in him again, not caring if it hurt him or not.

He was the bottom. Take this dick, handle it. A true bottom could take dick with his eyes closed while bungee jumping towards a tight rope in a tutu. I looked at my watch and decided I had to get back home. It was 4:45 a.m.

My girl's alarm was set for 5 a.m., and she loved waking up and sucking my dick and I loved head so I strained my muscles and I caught a nut instantly, coming inside him. I put on my clothes and hopped in my car.

"We can't at least talk?"

"I gotta get home. We'll hook up later."

He lets me out and I burn rubber. When I got home I cut the engine and rushed through the front door, closing it. I put in her birthday and the door chime activated without making a sound. I inhaled, getting high off his scent on my top lip. I loved the way he smelled. I loved him. I wanted to be with him again. Fucking him opened everything I had suppressed.

When I got to the room I was happy that she's still sleeping. I take a quick shower and dry off. Brushing my teeth, I then crawl in bed beside her, looking in her face. I felt guilty, but at the same time if she learned how to treat me better I would treat her better.

I loved watching her sleep. I sat there until the alarm sounded and I pretended I was sleep. She fumbled all over the sheets and her hands find my dick. She gripped it and I held my breath. She pulled it out and sucked on it; it started to grow in her mouth. Her warmth was pleasant and I closed my eyes, imagining she was Luscious. In contrast, she used her tongue to form circles on my rod. Luscious used those very same circular motions but he deep throats in ways that blew my mind.

She smiled at me, trying to fully awaken.

"I can't wait to marry you," she said, making me feel good. I didn't want to marry her at all, but I'm on the Low, I have to do this.

Damn it. "I can't wait, either."

"My cousin, Elroy, should be in town. He's staying with a friend of mine who just bought a house not too far from here."

Ask me do I give a fuck! I held her head, loving her moist mouth and the way she pulled on my balls.

"Oh, yeah?"

She started to slowly kiss my nuts and that felt good. She took the left nut into her mouth, humming a tune.

"Yes. He's been having bad luck. He got HIV and he is in denial about it."

I didn't want to hear about this.

"Sorry to hear that."

"Damn, you taste good, baby."

Can you please hurry up! "Thanks."

"I'm going to see him later on today, do you wanna come?"

I tensed up and I curled my toes. I was about to come and my girl loved to swallow.

I was stuttering. "Sure…anyways, what's his name?"

She sucked on my balls, giving me a head rush. Cum spurted from my dick and in the air and she started wiping it up and sucking it from her fingers. She put some in my mouth and I tasted it.

"His name is…" Slurp, slurp. "George Samuels."

My dick went soft in her mouth and I had heart failure.

*Yes. He's been having bad luck. He got HIV and he is in denial about it…*Oh my God! And I swallowed him. And my girl just swallowed me.

We're now infected…

I can never tell her. I will take it to my grave.

THE ATOMIC BOMB

I had a bad dream. A very, very bad dream. Of my father. He was chasing me through legions of roses, out in some field during some unknown time. Huge numbers descended upon my head, like a countdown, slowly counting to something. But what? The beginning of life? My death? Who knew? Oblivious to my bleeding hands, I was looking over my shoulder, panting and trying to survive. He had a huge machete knife, swinging, sending rose petals flaking towards the ground that became flames. My shoes became ashes, my feet started to blister horribly. I was screaming against smoke blowing in my face like a dragon was in front of me.

"DAD STOP!"

He was relentless, evil...cunning.

"I'M GOING TO KILL YOU!"

I could not believe my eyes and ears.

"DAD STOP!"

Out of nowhere a cliff appeared, and I had to stop. Turning, I held up my hands in fear as the machete fell against my shoulder, snapping away claws of a demon I didn't see. I was aghast, about to faint. He started stomping the demon.

"Leave my son alone! He's my heir, my heir, if only he wasn't a homo...."

Abruptly, I sat up from a deep sleep, dripping in sweat. I had jumped out of bed as if it was on fire, swinging my fists like someone tried to kill me, punching holes in the walls as if my life depended on it. My eyes wide, my heart was about to beat out of my chest. When I realized I was in my room I started to calm down.

"What the fuck...?"

My naked, sweaty body seemed tired, beat up. I was on fire, literally. I could barely catch my breath let alone grasp a thought.

Did I read into the dream?

Or did I forget it?

I knew I couldn't forget it because I have been having the same dream for three years now.

And it started when I found my father dead with a liquor bottle in his hand, an empty Tylenol bottle by his side and a blunt razor resting tenderly on his suede-clad lap.

The same razor he used to slit his own neck.

I stirred slightly. I wasn't in a deep sleep. It was the state of rest where you knew you were awake but your eyes were still closed and you could hear the sounds of your house flowing into your ears like melted butter. You wanted to move but you didn't because you were so relaxed. The bed felt like a good massage table, your body seemed at peace...I had on silk panties…I loved wearing them to bed, but you couldn't pay me to tell anybody that. It was a secret I would take to my grave.

My dick was so hard it throbbed, sending surges of pleasure throughout my body like hurricane victims escaping a storm. The relief befell me like a lover picking flowers. My hands came alive as I reached for the lotion bottle. I didn't open my eyes, I knew where everything was. I slept with the lotion bottle under my pillow. I jacked off every single solitary morning, whether a warm body was next to me or not.

I squeezed a moderate amount in my hands, rubbing them together. I loved jacking off; it made me feel calm, good and beautiful. It relaxed me and my soul. I loved doing it solo, I never allowed anyone to help me get off. It lost its power if you handed it over to another individual. Just what floated my boat. It'd never change.

I started at the head, working my right hand over the swelling until a moan escaped my lips. I was wiggling my hips, my dick passing through the O shape I made with my hand. I nearly passed out from the sudden pleasure. My legs begin to tremble with a preamble unknown to my toes. I flowed into myself. Motioned my spirit. My heat rose. My cold air fell. I tried to free Egypt from bondage. I was all across the king-sized bed, my nuts bouncing like Jordan trying to win the sixth championship ring. I was moaning to myself, imagining Shemar Moore kissing all over my swelling nipples. He took the left one into his mouth as his soft hands worked my abs, chest…trailed down to my torso.

I never been with a man, touched a man in a sexual way. I was never abused as a kid, I was never mishandled. I wasn't born gay; I just saw one too many male-to-male interactions growing up in my uncle's home. He was gay, but on the Down Low with it. No one in town had a clue. He got pussy like 1-2-3. He had hoes sucking his dick like A-B-C. When he thought I was asleep he'd bring in his male lovers, all thug types from other states, and they'd fuck him so good I heard him through the walls. He never fucked dudes in his back yard. He didn't wanna play the Bating Cage Game in his own hometown. I'd run to his room as a curious, easily impressionable eleven-year-old and crack open the door. He was being gang banged, man handled. He acted like he loved it. My dick got hard. It turned me on. I didn't know men did it with men, never knew it. My dad at the time told me men did it with women, he never brought up the subject of bisexuality or homosexuality. I knew then I wanted to experience the pleasure.

My uncle used to say, "Oh that dick feel so good niggah, tap that ass, damn boy take that booty..."

They had him in the doggy. Missionary-style. On his back with his legs pushed back. He'd have on unlaced boots every time. Uncle Lloyd liked it like that. They got the ass raw dog, meaning without protection.

That did it for me, but I never acted on it. Now Shemar Moore, in my mind of course, was kissing me, getting on top of me, ready for me. He spread himself open as I slid into him, his tight soul gripped at my shaft wanting comfort. And I would give it to him. Cool air blew across my body as I felt the warmth on my dick, a slick tongue trailing the incredible lengths. I felt lips and tongue kissing my scrotum, sending me up the wall. Hands gripped my chest, squeezing my muscles hard as a hot mouth fucked my dick until a jerk snapped in my toes. I was about to die in heaven. I wanted to fuck the angels while I was up here.

The atomic bomb built in the core of my soul, ready for activation…the bases stocked up, the soldiers put on their uniforms and picked up their weapons. The world was listening as my soldiers engaged in combat throughout Hiroshima and Nagasaki…My spine was exploding as my hips twirled like war jets. The target locked as Shemar's hot mouth descended on my dick and the tip of it brushed against his quivering tonsils. Out. In. Out. In. Oooout. Iiiiiin. Out. Paused. Hands slapped my thighs. In.

Yea, niggah. Fuck that dick with that hot mouth.

Seconds began to unfold. The countdown began. Roses in my mind. Flames in my loins. The ground shook beneath my bed. I was moaning and panting, gripping Shemar's head. Yea, baby. Yea. I'm 'bout to cum! I love to come, please hurry up and make me come. Hiroshima and Nagasaki merged into one as his tongue manipulated the human population trapped in my cum as it spurt from the hole of my throbbing dick and I dug my nails into my pillow, loving Shemar, wanting Shemar, needing Shemar.

When it subsided I took in a deep breath, damn near going blind. I kept my eyes closed as the cool air vanished. I slowly came to, opening my eyes, looking around my room. I was drenched with sweat.

Not a sign of my cum anywhere.

Quietly, I was feeding my son some cereal, trying not to think about the dream let alone my father's death. I loved Father, and my heart went into some sort of mental transition for the worst when he was found in the critical state he was in. I missed him, loved and adored him. I found myself sometimes looking over the memories we shared now forever captured in the form of framed photographs placed some of everywhere in my home.

Facing the end of my tether, I was sitting down at my dining table, enjoying the little sunshine coming through my lace-curtain-clad window. Little sun shapes were on my arm. It was hot in here and I should turn on the A.C. but my light bill was sixty dollars higher last month so I have been using the ceiling and store-bought fans. Waste of money, actually, because if it was hot inside all the fans did was blow hot air so I wound up leaving them off. To distract myself from the dream and Daddy, I opened the Sunday paper and started to take out the coupons.

My body felt good, despite my ill-thoughts. I found myself biting a nail and smiling, looking coyly at the ads. Closing my eyes a sudden rush of lust fancifully danced through my nerves, settling in my blood stream.

I felt it pumping through my heart and electrifying my eyes.

There I was putting lotion in my hands. In my bed. This morning. Just after my dream. I felt good. Sensational. My dick was rising like the sun. My inhibition setting like the sun. Started at the head. Working it. I was smiling, putting the paper in front of my face. There was Shemar Moore. Loving me, needing me, throbbing for me. His insides were my most sacred place.

"Daddy, why are you so quiet?" my son asked me, the instant I started to come. In shock, because I hadn't even touched myself to feel this urge, this explosion, I closed my eyes shut.

"Daddy are you ok?"

I faked it. "My stomach hurts."

"You gotta use the toilet, huh?" he asked, making me laugh through my lingering orgasm.

"Naw, nothing like that sport."

He looked at me when I set the paper down. "You sure, Daddy?"

I gave him a hard glance, had to remind him that I was his Daddy and not his son.

"I am cool, Jr."

"Oh, ok. Be stubborn, Daddy."

My cum, cold on my thigh, was driving me crazy (in a bad way). I attempted to stand up and go clean myself but I quickly sat back down because cum had soaked through my pants.

Outraged I yelled, "FUCK!"

My son's head snapped in my direction.

"Daddy, you cussing."

"Sorry." *Why did I cum like that? What is wrong with me? I'm not gay and I'm sitting here thinking of Shemar Moore, what the fuck, yo. Am I going crazy? Going through some type of black man phase where I don't know where I'm going and what or who I'm doing? Do I need to see a shrink?*

He smiled at me. He loved me with all his heart. "Still don't want to tell me what's wrong?"

Rubbing his head I said, "Maybe when you're older."

"Whatever, Daddy."

The Locked Room

A hurricane in my heart, I watched her when she walked through the door. She barely closed it. Her head low, she sucked in air and looked up into my eyes. We stared. We blinked. I smiled. She frowned. She seemed to be in a bad mood. I knew why, of course. She was the type of woman who wanted everyone to spoil her. She wanted this out the stores; if we had bills to pay she'd fuck over the light bill for some high heels out of Bloomingdale's. She wanted people to say she's "pretty," "gorgeous" and "pretty gorgeous." I wasn't with the program. She was my lady and yes I ate that pussy and I cooked for her, sometimes washing her clothes. But I would not inflate her head with bullshit.

Rolling her pretty eyes at me, she dropped her purse on the floor. "Hi," she said, kicking off her heels.

I flipped through channels on the TV, holding my dick. "Hey."

Her hands on her hips, she asked, "Is that all you have to say?"

I sipped my Heineken.

"*Yeeep.*"

Damn these silk pajama pants were irritating my damn nuts.

She tucked her chin back, taking off her coat.

"Yep?"

"Yes, baby, damn. Don't start."

She opened the closet door, hanging her coat on an iron hanger.

"Why do you act like we aren't having problems?"

I looked at her. I meant business.

"We're having a *problem.* In the singular form."

She rolled her eyes and sat on the opposite chair. That hurt my feelings, that she wouldn't sit by me but I hid it from my face. When she wanted me to eat her pussy she always sat in my lap. When she wanted this dick in her ass she knew how to purr like a mountain lion on my balls. Now she's too good for me. "It's going to be in the plural form soon."

"Please. You're just mad because I won't tell you you're beautiful twenty times a damn day."

"What?"

"Yes. It started last week. You kept walking your big ass in front of me, asking me 'Am I sexy? Am I pretty?'

Yes, you are but damn why do I have to say it twenty-four hours a day?"

"Because you're my man."

"Right. We are committed. We pay bills, well I pay the majority of them. I let you keep your money. You are automatically beautiful to me. You are my queen. Those niggahs at your job got you feeling all hot and cute and you better tell those niggahs to chill because Survivor Island: Beijing will be held in their ass when I kick them to sleep."

"You're so jealous," she said, standing up and stretching.

I put my hands in my boxers and squeezed my balls and closed my eyes. I was apprehensive.

"Of what? That's my pussy! You're my woman. This is your dick."

"Wow. Big deal."

"Grow up. You're always starting senseless arguments. Your day is fucked so you fuck up my goddamn day."

"Don't use the Lord's name in vain."

"You use my dick in vain every time I blow your back out making your cum run down my nuts."

"You're so romantic, jeez!"

I glared at her.

"Chill, woman."

"I have a name," she sassed me.

I shook my head. Fuck this beer -- I needed some Grey Goose and a joint.

"Why are you so argumentative?"

"Because it's been a long time since you said I'm pretty," she said, totally confusing me.

"You fucking Cancers kill me, moody ass."

"And you're a Cancer too, water bucket."

"I'm going to bed."

"I'm sleeping on the couch," she said.

Then I stood up and slid my ashy feet into my black slippers. Wolfing down the rest of the beer I retreated to my room and grabbed a pillow. Walking back out to her I threw it at her and it hit her in the head.

"FINE, GOOD NIGHT."

And I retired to my room and closed the door, locking it.

At 2 a.m. she bammed on the door. I heard her, in fact her bamming startled me but I didn't feel like moving.

"Baby, I'm horny."

I was horny as hell too. She had some good pussy but I was in love with her. Sex wasn't everything. Her happiness and taking care of her rated higher than putting my big dick in her. I could always get the pussy, sure. But I wanted her heart. I wanted her to understand that I cared for her and I would fight for her and die for her.

I snored louder, smiling in my sleep and hugging the pillow.

"BABY! OPEN THE DOOR!"

I opened my right eye. The Vaseline bottle came into focus. I was rock hard. I must have been dreaming about fucking Beyonce again and making Jay-Z wipe up my cum from the sheets.

"I'm tired…"

"This is my room too. Open the damn door. I wanna fuck!"

"I wanna love you."

"FUCK LOVE! Put your dick in me and make me your dirty little slut!"

"I don't want my lady talking like that."

"PLEASE!"

"No. I am with you because I love you."

"Bullshit. You didn't say that last week when I gave you some pussy when you had a bad day at the office."

"Did I ask for it?"

"No, but…"

"But shut the fuck up! I'm trying to goddamn sleep!"

"OPEN THIS DOOR!"

She was kicking it.

I love it! She's getting upset. She doesn't get her way and suddenly the world ends.

"Beg for this dick!"

"OPEN THE DOOR! I wanna be fucked, baby, damn!"

"No." I grabbed the Vaseline, taking off the blue top.

"Why?"

"Because you haven't said that I'm handsome," I joked, playing her game.

"YOU'RE HANDSOME! YEA! A REAL DENZEL!"

I was offended. "Denzel is old as fuck. Why can't I be Morris Chestnut."

"Because he's fine and you're…I'm sorry baby."

"WHAT?"

She was punching the door. "Open the door. I'm sorry. I'll make it up to you!"

I saw her panties on the bed. I could smell her pussy from here. I picked them up and rubbed my face in her essence. I loved her scent.

"Open the door, damn baby! Fuck!"

I rubbed Vaseline all over my hands. I sighed, preparing my dick for the covenant. I gently stroked my dick, starting from the swollen mushroom head and making my way to the base of my nuts. It felt so incredible. Then, opening my legs, I put her panties on my face and closed my eyes.

"Open the door, man."

The smell of her pussy and perfume rendered me speechless. Gyrating my hips all over the silk sheets, the hairs on my ass kept sticking to the silk and it stung, but it was a good stinging, mixed with the joyous pleasure I brought myself.

"Damn this shit feels good," I cooed, loud enough for her to hear.

She was appalled.

"What are you doing? I know you're not masturbating."

I pulled on my balls, deeply inhaling her pussy, sucking on the panties. My nipples were erect and I was floating through the sky like Anne Rice vampires, wanting to fuck Lestat because my girl was insecure.

I wanted Akasha, from Queen of the Damned, to bite into my neck, make me her fledgling. Take me. I want to be one with the Blood, with the darkness.

"Damn, I'm about to come. This feels so good. Inhaling your pussy from these panties and jacking my dick!"

She pounded on the door.

"Open the door."

I never knew I could make myself feel so great.

"This feels better than your pussy baby!"

"I'ma kick down this fucking door!"

The pleasure wrapped the tunnels of my mind and started explosions along my limbs, settling in my loins…making me scream out. I inhaled faster, using my tongue to put the panties in my mouth. I was fucking my hand, my dick sliding against the Vaseline.

"Oh, God. Here it comes!"

I came so hard I fell out the bed.

"I hate you! Open the door."

Her panties on my pillow, I inhaled her pussy, until I fell asleep.

And I didn't tell her good night.

I left her spoiled ass pounding on the door.

Closed until Further Notice

I was hanging out with my home girl Plausia. She pushed her purse aside. "You haven't touched your food."

I picked up the crafty-looking fork with roses on the handle and toyed with my cold shrimp pasta. "I'm not hungry."

She studied me. I hated being examined.

"Why? What's going on?"

"It's my dude. He is a stubborn asshole."

"Welcome to Hell, Gurl."

"I know, right. Where's Satan, so I can see where the buffet is at…"

"What did he do?"

I sipped my Sprite. I wasn't an alcoholic bitch. Ladies Night at the Clubs didn't make my pussy wet.

"It's a question of what he hasn't done."

"He must not be fucking you right."

"How did you know?"

"He's my ex-boyfriend, remember. And he can't fuck that great. Sometimes he doesn't know what to do with pussy. Frame it, eat it, fuck it, sauté it or shoot it…"

"*Amen*, Girl!" We slapped palms. "So be it, so motherfucking be it. *Chile*, I got rug burn on my knees and he didn't even make my pussy fart."

She chocked on her drink. "You're a *mess*, Chile."

"He can eat a mean steak, I tell you. He made my pussy feel like a T-bone. All I needed was some Welch's grape juice to seal the deal. But his *real* bone I wouldn't throw to my pit bull. She'd throw the bone back and be like, '*Bitch*, stop playing with me.'"

We chuckled. She pulled her short hair into a ponytail and flipped through her unanswered text messages on her cell phone.

"Have you talked to him?"

"Plausia, he's your ex so of course you know talking to a brick wall only gets you migraines."

"Yes. I know, Gurl."

"He feels he's the best. His ego is so far up his ass he can't smell his own shit because his nose is nowhere near his rectum."

"Gurl, you got a way with words. But still try to talk to him. He's sweet. He isn't a bad guy."

"I know. But how do you tell your man that you have been faking orgasms for three fucking years?"

"Damn. It's been *that* long?"

"Yes, ma'am. If it wasn't for the power of masturbation and vibrators my cum would be barrels of dust."

We chuckled.

"Well, my advice to you is to talk to him."

"I can't. *That* will fail."

"Then write him a note. And put it somewhere you know he'll find it."

I thought about it. I actually smiled.

My dude talked a lot of shit and thought he was going to fuck me. Why did men do that? Some of them took the submissive thing as a woman's weakness, yet he wore my panties more than I did. I didn't sweat it because he was my man and I knew he wasn't gay. If you wanted to wear my panties then go for it. I loved a freaky ass man and seeing his fine ass wearing my panties turned me on. But the way he talked to me sometimes pissed me off. Just because you stick the pussy doesn't mean you run shit. Especially when you didn't pay any bills. If you're a man don't think you're going to lay up in my house, eat my food, fart up the air, shit all day and smoke up my weed and drink my liquor. Go get your broke ass a J-O-B. When I went to work I didn't let anybody stay in my crib. My home was a Home, not a Rest Stop. Waffles-n-Things restaurant was ninety miles north of my home. Everybody gotta leave when Mama Mia wasn't home.

Granted, I didn't want a man I could control. I wasn't into toys and the only remote control I wanted was for my TV and DVD player. I didn't respect men who let their women run them. We all had our roles to play and I would never step on his manhood but he was pussyfooting and stepping on my *pussy*hood by not making me come. I hadn't come with him -- ever. And that was sad because if the wind blew I would come without touching myself. My Inhibition Levels were at an all-time high dealing with him.

Then he loved to piss me off. Just so he could have make-up sex. If you wanted to have make-up sex there was a much easier way. I'll put on some makeup and lipstick – then we fuck. *See* there! Makeup sex. *Voila,* goddamn it. With his stroke less ass. I mean…get *real*, dude. He had some good tongue. But his dick was trash. That's what I get for not test driving the Honda before I settled for the fully-loaded Buick. The Buick didn't come with an air bag, free oil changes or a jack when the tires went flat. His radiator blew and the handle blew my pussy. I called Triple A but they were like, "Bitch, *please*." Now I was stuck making payments on a Buick that couldn't last a mile in the bedroom.

As a woman why did I have to break my back while he was trying to blow *my* back out? That made no sense.

I was supposed to lay on my back or put my face down and my pussy up and he was supposed to dig in my ass, like my thong underwear, and grip my ass cheeks and beat my pussy, then pull out and suck his dick off my vaginal walls like I was being steam-cleaned.

That made absolutely no sense to me. I was panting and sweating more than *he* was and he was supposed to knock the dust off my pussy and he wound up knocking everything off the dresser, even the lamp, and *still* couldn't make my pussy come like a Trick Daddy song. This pissed me off so badly I went out and bought a dildo and started fucking myself because, let's be real. I *loved* my man. I would do anything for love. But goddamn it, I won't do *that*! -- pretend anymore. I was the singer Meat Loaf and I was tired of faking orgasms! I wasn't going to be like the other Hoes and dump him just because he wasn't that skilled in the bedroom. You didn't fuck over a good man like that. He was very compassionate, loved the elderly and he would give the shirt off his back for people. He treated me like a queen, always got my hair and nails done and gave me naked, full body massages.

He just couldn't fuck and when I tried to teach him he shut down like a whore's pussy after a hard day's work and wasn't responsive. That's when he was the typical stubborn man, saying NO to everything I suggested.

So I did something especially for him. I waited until he got off work and I called his phone. He answered. "Hey, Baby."

"Hurry home. I can't wait to see you."

He chuckled seductively.

"Are you craving this dick?"

Um, No! "Yes, baby. I got the pussy cleaned for you."

"I'ma eat that shit good."

Um, No! "Sure, baby. How is the traffic?"

"Monstrous, but I should be home in about forty minutes."

"I'll be waiting."

"I can't wait to bask in your warmth."

"I can't wait to feel you."

Um, No!

I hung up. *I'm tired of being sucked. I want him to dick me down into the ground.*

Doo Doo Brown, Uncle Luke style.

I put on a Jane Fonda workout video and did some aerobics, tiring myself out. I did some sit ups and six sets of crunches until my stomach was sore. I ate a few bananas and decided to play with my pussy. Drenched in sweat I rubbed my sexy self into an orgasm about ten minutes later.

I took a quick shower and got out; knowing me and my dude would get into it later because I decided to keep the pre-historic dinosaurs in the kitchen. Meaning I didn't cook a motherfucking thing. I didn't restock his beer, even though he rarely drank. I left the fridge on empty status. He told me to go grocery shopping and he gave me $400. I put the money in my bank account and threw the grocery list in the trash. I didn't wash his clothes. If he couldn't fuck me right then why should I play Martha Stewart Living? I'd let her ass fuck me if she grew a pair and knew how to use it.

I kept the clothes in the laundry room. I didn't mop the floor. I left his clothes strewn throughout the bedroom. I shut down like a whore's pussy after a day of work just like he had when I was willing to teach him how to stroke it right. No one knew my pussy better than I did. All of the aforementioned things were serious pet peeves of his.

I would never cheat on him. I loved him too much. If I had to cheat I'd dump him but I didn't want to leave because he was my universe and with HIV and STDs on the rise I needed to keep my man.

I wrote a note and tied it around my booty cheeks. I then sprayed on some Victoria's Secret. Smiling at my gorgeous, toned body in the mirror I slid into a skimpy black dress that barely covered my ass. I thought I was slick. I got him thinking I was waiting up for him and I purposely tired myself out just so I could do one thing before he came home.

I lay in the bed and I fell asleep on my stomach.

Gillette Farmer walked into his home and said, "Georgica, where are you?"

The house was silent. Smiling, he locked and closed the door.

"I know she cooked."

He waltzed into the kitchen, proud of the woman he had and turned on the lights. Nothing was cooked. He inhaled deeply, looking around wildly.

He could have sworn tumbleweeds rolled across the black and white checkered tile.

Damn it. Where was she?

He took off his dirty work uniform and left on the boxers. He smelled like work and ass. He worked his ass off today, paint stripping Florida's roads.

He threw the clothes on the floor and looked around his huge laundry room.

Clothes were in the dirty clothes hamper. Noting was washed.

"What the fuck?"

Ж

He turned out the lights and walked to his room. When he entered he smiled, looking at his woman. She had on a short, skimpy dress. She slept soundly. But then the sight of his clothes everywhere arrested his attention and his hands became fists.

"What the hell have you been doing all day…and I thought you were waiting up for me to get this dick."

He sat beside her and leaned down to her face.

He kissed her cheek and watched her sleep for a few moments, his heart fluttering at the sight of her amazing ass.

I should slide up in the pussy while she's sleep. She always sucked my dick when I was sleeping. Why not return the favor?

He started to slip his hand up her dress and he felt a paper.

Looking confused, he lifted her dress and there was a huge paper tied to her pleasantly plump ass.

Like a billboard.

Sorry. We're closed until further notice.
Learn to perfect your craft and we'll open again.
Hurry now.
Jack your dick or something because you're
not stroking the pussy right.
Sorry for the inconvenience.

He stood up, angry. He glared at her and sat on the chair, turning on the TV. He cursed her so bad he had to close his eyes. His ego was seriously bruised.

He sat there until he fell asleep.

When she awakened Gillette was sitting beside her on the bed. She stretched and yawned; he had showered and had on a robe and her panties. It was tied closed.

"Hey," she said.

He didn't want to look at her.

"Are you mad with me?" she asked.

"Yes."

"Why?"

"You stood me up."

"I didn't mean to." *Yes I did.*

"I am horny for you."

"I'm *not* horny for you."

His mouth fell open.

"And why didn't you cook?"

"Why haven't you made me come in three years?"

His mouth fell open.

"What is this about?"

"It's about not giving you what you want. It's about having fifty-fifty in a relationship."

He laughed in her face.

"And I did make you come – over and over."

He grinned, holding his dick. "Didn't we?" he asked it.

I slapped it and he winced, jumping out of his skin.

I spat icily, "I faked it. I faked orgasms for three years because I didn't wanna hurt your feelings. You need to learn how to compromise."

"No."

"Ok. See our clothes? They stay on the floor. See how clean the kitchen is? It will stay that way because I am not cooking you a motherfucking thing."

She stood up and snatched the note from her ass.

She glared at him.

"My booty cheeks and my pussy meant what they said. 'We're closed until further notice.' I will not fuck you at all if you refuse to grow in the aspect of your sex life that has become such lackluster bullshit. I feel like I gotta go fuck a dyke bitch."

"Baby…"

She hurt his feelings and it showed on his face.

"I mean it."

"But why now?" he whined.

"Because you're getting beside yourself. For real, Man. I can only do so much. I can only take so much. You pushed the envelope and I'm about to give you a postage stamp. Shit gotta change and shit gotta change overnight."

"I'm sorry, Baby. But I don't have to do anything I don't want to do."

"Ok. Is that how you feel?"

"Yes."

"Good. I will do what the fuck I want. I will *not* wash clothes. I am not going grocery shopping. Do it yourself. I am moving out and moving with my mother until you learn to collaborate with me. I am with you to get all things. I shouldn't have to fuck myself to get my kind of pleasure. That's your job. If I want you digging in my pussy then motherfucker dig deep."

He got out of bed and hugged her.

"OK, baby. You win. When shall we start? You can teach me. What am I doing wrong? How can I make you come?"

"By making love to my mind."

She hugged her man. Her plan worked.

She called Plausia.

"Sup, Chile."

Georgica wiped sweat from her face, basking in the glow of her first orgasm. And it wasn't from him eating her out.

"I fucking love you."

"Why?"

She still felt tiny tremors that seemed to settle in her titties. "I wrote him a note and he listened."

"You're kidding."

"I'm serious. He has literally become a stallion. He even let me show him how I like my pussy stroked. And he practiced. But I gotta go. He wants to practice again. Ciao. He's mine now, bitch."

CLICK!

The Basketball Court

I was driving up Palm Drive, headed for Princeton Park. I was going to take the short cut to Homestead through the neighborhood. I didn't normally go this way but traffic along 112th Avenue was horrendous since they opened a new school and tore down nearly every tree to build new communities and a CVS drug store.

I signaled left when I approached the four-way stop and I braked. Coming to a complete stop I let a man driving a Ford go ahead of me, since he was in a rush.

Fucking Cubans, I tell you. Making the left I approached the park and noticed the plethora of dope boy, thug niggahs and regular pretty boys playing basketball on the court. So many cars out here it looked like a free concert.

A few niggahs were bar-be-queing and I decreased in speed, taking in the legions of honeys prancing by with tight coochie huggers and halter tops, weave out of this world and high heels, looking sexy. I rolled down the window, came to a halt and said, "Hey, girl." One of them looked with a smile.

"Sup, baby, can a niggah get a moment of your time?"

She walked over to my car sucking a lollipop suggestively.

"Sup, Pa. What's going on with you?"

"I'm chill, try'na see what's good with you. How about taking a ride with me?"

"Come on, Brenda," her friend said with an attitude.

"Wait girl, I got this. Give me your number, Pa. I'll meet up with you after the game."

She leaned into my face and kissed my cheek. I looked at her with a sly smile. Yeah. I pulled Hoes like that.

I took her cell and typed my number in, saving it under Pimp Daddy.

"Pimp Daddy. I like that."

"You do? I like those pretty titties, Ma. Damn, making my mouth water."

"Well, call me in about an hour."

A car was honking at me. I slowly mashed the gas pedal and before I could pass the park I noticed a sexy man looking my way. Signaling right, I turned onto some side street, parked by a green SUV with the spinning rims and cut the engine.

I was enjoying the game. Sexy niggahs clad in basketball shorts of assorted sizes. Sticking to their sweaty asses – what a pretty sight. So much dick was jumping, jumping, I thought I was at the meat store about to order

Plan #7, the most expensive one. Part of me was in an outrage because I wasn't gay, so why was I sitting here looking at the boys like that? Getting aroused when one of them slapped another's ass and that booty bounced. Goddamn. My dick was brick.

Some had their shirts off. I saw beer guts wobbling on the elder ones, and tight chests and killer abs on some of the younger ones. They talked shit loudly and a couple dudes looked like they were beefing. I found it funny. I turned on the radio and chilled, smoking a Kool cigarette.

A tall dude with long dreadlocks pulled into a rubber band made the game winning shot. Swish. Nothing but net. His fade away was admirable. People slapped his ass and he slapped palms, walked over to the bleachers to grab his towel and a water jug and walked towards me.

I froze.

His swagger killed me, so masculine. People called his name and he spoke with a smile. He was about 6 feet 8, his feet looked a size 15. He didn't wear underwear and that snake slithered all over his thigh. He looked me directly in the eyes, licked his lips absent-mindedly then grabbed his dick, pulling on it as if to free it and when he released it…it thumped against his thigh with a jerk that made me get harder. He was packing better than Vienna sausages.

Disgruntled about the entire situation, I pushed down on my dick and bit my tongue to bring myself pain so it would deflate.

Why was gay shit on my mind? I had never been with a dude in my life, never even thought about it. I detested punks -- didn't want 'em around me for me or doing shit to me. I didn't listen to gay songs, I didn't wear any color that made up the Pride Rainbow Coalition, if you wanted to call it that, and I damn sure could pull hoes.

He was closer. Dick bouncing. Still looking at me.

Turning on Bob Marley, I closed my eyes so hard I thought I snapped a migraine I didn't know I had in the base of my medulla. I counted to ten. One Mississippi…two Mississippi…three.

When I got to ten my dick was getting soft. Good. Opening my eyes I was shocked to see homeboy sitting on the hood of my $23,000 automobile watching another basketball game in progress. He was cackling on his cell phone, like he didn't have a care in the world. The sun was about to set. The trees all around me began shaking branches because the breeze picked up. I was mesmerized me with this Greek God on my hood – fine motherfucker. Nah, niggah. Take that back. You didn't look at men and think they were fine. That's crazy, something was wrong with me.

What did I do? Niggahs down south were a crazy breed and would shoot you quick if you got jiggy with it.

I studied him as I continued to breathe deeply. My body tingled and my nipples hardened. Sweat trickled down his back (a huge tattoo of a dragon covered almost the entire length of his back) and was running into the crack of his magnificently shaped butt.

My boy called me again and I answered. "Dawg, where are you? I'm about to go if you don't hurry up and you can catch me tomorrow."

"Niggah I got caught up, just wait for me, please dawg."

I hung up and blew my horn. He looked back at me with a smile, bringing the phone from his lips. They were parted, showing off the gleam of his clean-looking pearly white teeth.

Good hygiene, Ow, baby!

"Mind getting your big ass off my goddamn ride, dawg? Fucking up my paint job."

He spoke into the phone and hung it up, walking around to my car door. I looked at him and he looked at me, his dick all in my face. TV-shape dipped into the shorts just the way I loved. Hell, it was then I realized why I loved watching ESPN so much: the fine men.

He knocked on the window.

I didn't roll it down. I reached under my seat for my piece (my shiny pistol).

He knocked again and I rolled it down. He greeted me with a smile.

"Sorry, dawg. I didn't know someone was in here."

I felt like shit. So he didn't notice me, and he wasn't looking into my eyes. Oh, well. Good. Now I wasn't horny anymore. I was clearly embarrassed.

"No problem."

"You see my game winning shot, nice fade away, huh?" he asked, extending his hand. "I'm Gerald."

"Sup, Gerald. That was pretty hot."

"That's my SUV right there you're parked next to."

"Really? So you prop your big ass on my ride?"

"Yea, dawg. Can I sit in there with you? Lemme ask you something."

Hell, yea. But I down played it, couldn't give him a big head, no pun intended.

"Sure."

He opened the passenger side door and got in my ride. He looked like a sardine in a can, but he let the seat back. He was breathing uncontrollably, his abs flexing, turning me on. I rolled the window back up, cranked the car and turned on the AC.

"Thanks, homie."

"No problem."

"So where are you from? And are these police tints on your ride? Aren't they illegal?"

"I'm from here. Yea, they're police tints."

"Hell, I know. I am a cop, I was asking."

A cop? Oh, Lord. And I got a gun in my ride. I got a little fidgety.

"Don't arrest a niggah."

He looked at me, studying me. "I'ma be real with you. I think you're kinda fly."

"And I guess you're the can of Raid."

He laughed, patting my knee. "You got jokes."

"And you got dick."

I covered my mouth, averting his face. I wanted to run. "Sorry, dawg that didn't come out right."

He was looking at me seductively, rubbing his big dick. I shook with fear because I was about to branch off into the unknown but I wanted it, welcomed it. Up until this point my life had been pretty familiar. Get up every morning. Shower. Cook eggs and grits. Make up my bed, tidy the room. Go to work. Call Mama. Deal with bullshit people and my crummy boss. Go to lunch. Buy something. Go back to work. Clock out hours later. And drive home. If I wasn't tired maybe I'd masturbate.

He leaned up to me, those thick lips inches from my quivering ones. He kissed me, looking in my eyes, giving me some tongue. Slow tongue. I was holding his dick, squeezing it.

I pulled it out, going for the juggler. I went down on him, running my tongue all over it. It was a pretty dick; I never knew it could look so appealing to the senses. I didn't know what the hell to do – I just did what came to mind. I sucked on the head and he cooed. Grabbing my head he was all about taking his time. He smelled good; I smelled the product of his hard labor on the court. I took another inch of dick into my mouth, carful not to get my teeth on it but I was new to the game and it happened anyway.

"You never sucked dick, dawg?" he asked, amused and turned on. His eyes sparkled.

"No."

"Take your time, homie. Take all the time you need on my dick." He was grinning. "Damn, I'm your first. That's hot, dawg…"

I took my time, working it, needing it and feeling it. After about ten minutes he locked up, and said, "Baby I'm about to come."

He took his dick from my mouth, grabbed me by the little hair I had, turned my face to the side of the head of his passion and he came all over my face, motioning his dick all over my closed eyes, nose and chin. I felt his slick tongue on my face, licking it up. He sucked my closed eyes, chin and nose, swallowing his own cum.

Goddamn that was hot.

"I'm not done with you yet," he said with a smile.

I didn't want him to be done either.

He was rubbing my thigh, trailing his huge hand up to my dick. Gripping it through the pants, he pulled it out and begins chopping me up, slowly working his jaws and tongue. I wanted to die. A man had never given me head.

He was moaning just the way I liked, sensually, low and barely audible. He played with my nuts and I loved the way he smelled. Gucci cologne mixed with sweat.

He deep throats my dick, taking it to the tonsils.

"Damn, dawg."

He looked up at me and said, "I'm going to unlock my SUV. Go get in it and wait for me."

With the quickness, I did so. When I closed the door to my car he unlocked his. I got inside, thankful it was huge in there and took into account homeboy had the best of all worlds in here. Porn movies. DVD screens. A PS3 hooked up in the back. A full bar in the back seat. He had the far back seat taken out and a little bed was in place of it. Baller shit.

About two minutes later he gets in the car and told me to get on the bed. I did so. He locked the car and didn't worry about people looking because everyone was focused on the game and we were a hundred feet away or so by the trees. No one saw us.

He had tints and curtains hanging. I loved it.

He took off his shorts, the dick dropping with gravity and left the Jordans on. He had on a small pair of light green panties. It didn't cover his dick or ass. I was about to nut on myself. He got in the back with me and got in the doggy style position. He handed me a condom, a Durex. I paused, scared a little bit. Homeboy had a nice ass and damn his brown rosebud looked so appealing. Since I ate the Hoes before, I ate him, running my tongue along the crevices, spreading his cheeks, the green panties stretching… and he moaned. He loved it. He shook that lime green panty-clad ass on my slick tongue. I was slapping his ass cheeks, getting possessive.

My dick harder than ever, I took off all my clothes, booty-butt naked and I put on the jimmy. I asked him was he relaxed.

"Yea, dawg. Do the damn thang. I got a wife to go home to."

I slid up in his tight hole, captured by the feeling. It felt so sensational I felt better than any woman ever made me feel. He was biting the little red pillow, gripping the mattress, throwing that ass on my dick. I gave him all nine inches.

"Damn. Boy. Damn. Baby. Take that shit, dawg." He was lost in my rhythm, we climbed the mountain together looking for the spring so we could drink our lust and reenergize our stamina and fall over into a blanket of ecstasy.

His ass jiggled all over me, the motion of the panties and ass hypnotizing me. Homeboy was throwing it as hard as I gave it. I straddled the booty and I crawled through this tall niggah, something opening up inside of me I couldn't grip, I couldn't see or understand but it understood me.

And I didn't understand it.

Before I could react, my body jerked as a sudden burning, delightful pleasure overcame me, crawling up my spine. Then licking my lips LLCool J-style, I grabbed his dreads and pulled them like reigns on a horse. I was slapping his ass with my left hand, making him take it.

"You like this dick?"

"I love that dick, damn."

"I'm going for the two points in the paint."

"You got three seconds."

"Two seconds…I'm about to nut, dawg!"

For the first time in my life I came in a condom, inside a man I would never see again.

When it subsided, I lay spent and homeboy took the condom, wiped my cum all over my dick and he began chopping me up.

Sweating hard, I thought to myself, "Hell yea, ole boy a freaky bitch."

My dick was ultra sensitive, but he got it up and he worked it out.

Closing my eyes I ignored Mack's ringtone as my phone came to life again.

I would never tell Mama or the boys about this.

I was officially on the Down Low.

Officially.

The Dressing Room

I was late getting to work today. I knew I shouldn't have gone out to the Club last night. I was 36-years-old, and tried to cling to my youth like leeches to skin trying to get some blood. My better self told me, NAH DUDE GO TO BED! YOU HAVE TO GET UP AT 7 a.m. AND MAKE SURE THE 401 (K) KEEPS TICKING 'CAUSE AIN'T SHIT FREE IN AMERIKKKA FOR A BLACK MAN!

But my Horny Self said, FUCK IT. NIGGAH DO YOU. AS A MATTER OF FACT BUY SOME LIQUOR, SOME BUD, and hump all night after the ailments take you to the Moon.

But before I talk about work, if I did talk about work, I always changed my mind. I had thoughts of this morning. I looked at the niggah right now. Naked. Uncensored. Exposed. In my bed. He is the first dude I ever brought home. Usually Hoes (females) made my home a Hotel-Motel-Holiday Inn giving them whatever they wanted 'cause I had it. The sun shined through the lacey curtains. The shapes all over his chest and the right side of his face – so angelic.

Around what? Three or four a.m? I was tossing and turning with someone. I felt his heat. His aura. His lust. Were vapors. Against my skin. I needed him. Wanted him. Longed for his trust. His passion. His seeds flowering my garden.

Shaking thinking about it, I remembered yesterday, I went to T.Q. Bax, 'cause a brothah's Platinum Card was nearly maxed out, and I bought a very cool-looking cream-colored cashmere sweater, since it was a little chilly right now in Miami. I had a closet filled with attire. You know a brothah could never have too much money, cash, liquor, bud or ass. I was dressed in some jeans that fit snuggly, not too tight, just enough to show the shape of the Booty and the Dick. My slides showed off pedicured toes. My white T-shirt I could have done without and the robe I had on, which was eight sizes too small, looked more like a robe/coat.

I remember a few months ago I saw a dude staring at me when I was driving. Why I thought of him at that particular moment beats the hell outta me. I tried to wave him down, to see if I knew him, but traffic was a bitch and I kept maneuvering around Cubans who couldn't drive to save Fidel Castro's life. It was a very muggy, humid day, I had fallen out with my boss over a meeting I had forgotten to schedule and I was set to send a manuscript off to publishers hoping I could get some sort of recognition but to no avail.

I never caught up with ole boy but the thought has eaten at me for some time. Why was the dude staring at me? Did he like me or what? Because I didn't do the fag shit.

As a matter of fact thinking about my robe/coat, I was looking over the sweater by the entrance of the pulsating-with-life store. Briefly I looked up and noticed the female section across the way. I had an eerie feeling that something wasn't right inside me. I couldn't put my finger on it. I went over to the female clothes and a big booty chick walked by, yapping on the phone. Yap yap yap, Girl and yap yap yap, No bitch yap yap yap.

I shook my head, looking at the booty for a minute, falling in love with the way it bounced in those Guess jeans.

I looked to my right and saw them – expensive satin panties. My mouth falling open, my dick was hard. There weren't many people and I was suddenly horny. I walked down one of the aisles, the racks chest level. I noticed the cameras everywhere. I closed my eyes, taking a pair of panties and smelling them. Wow. I unzipped my pants and crawled inside the rack of women's leather trench coats that hung to the floor…

Now this was crazy. I started stroking my dick with the panties, inhaling the leathery scent. A few women walked by chatting and I kept stroking, my nuts bouncing between my legs. I needed a nut badly! I'd never done this shit before but it felt so good, the adrenaline rushing to my head. My legs were trembling and tears escaped my eyes. Damn this shit felt good.

One of the jackets was whisked from the rack.

"This will look good on me girl, with my rhinestone pumps." She had blue weave and purple lips. Piercings were along her right ear and she wore tight black leather.

Another jacket left the rack and I was stuck, looking up at the women. They hadn't noticed me, dick out and panties in my hand. Damn it, I could hardly breathe. I didn't move a muscle, the beginnings of my orgasm subsiding back to the base of my nuts, telling the squirrels that their lunch break was over.

Another big girl saw me.

Her eyes wide, she was pointing excitedly.

"Oh my…"

I kicked her so hard in the shin she doubled into another rack, falling over. A few women rushed over to her and I got from behind the rack, grabbed a huge floral hat and pulled it low over my face. I fixed my pants. I was scared. That's what my dumb ass gets for stroking my stick in a store. I grabbed some sweat pants from the rack, rushed up the aisle and grabbed a man's shirt and jacket. I saw a baseball cap.

I went into the dressing room and changed clothing. I saw a plastic bag and I put my clothes in there, tossing the floral hat.

I left the dressing room, hat pulled low over my eyes.

"I swear! A man was jacking his dick with panties in the rack!"

"Yea, sure," said her friend, laughing at her.

"He kicked me!"

"Naw, those big ass titties wearing you down, lying bitch. You haven't had dick in months so you probably imagined a man jacking off."

"I swear!"

I dropped a hundred dollar bill to the cashier.

"That should pay for what I have on."

And I left the store, the sweat pants too damn tight around my balls.

I went to another store, towards the back of the mall. I found the nearest bathroom and splashed cold water on my face. I felt bad for kicking Miss Fat Butt but I had to. I put on my robe/coat and changed my pants. I felt much better getting out of those nut-busting ass sweat pants. I was looking over Echo shirts when a fine brothah came over to me with another fine brothah and said, "Damn that coat is the business."

He was 6 feet 1, masculine as he wanted to be. Nothing about him spelled G-A-Y. He had on a Tampa Bay jersey and his slacks hung low. Clean cut and smelled good.

His friend, who reminded me of someone, but I couldn't put my finger on it, extended his hand. "I'm Lloyd. I like that coat. Where did you buy it? They make robe/coats now?"

Shaking his hand firmly, I looked at him with a smile. I hated to smile but the niggah looked good. Damn. What was I saying? Why was I looking at ole boy like that? Was I going crazy or what? Brothah had it going on. He had some white in his blood because his hair was bushy yet thin and the freckles on his handsome face brought out his almond brown eyes.

"I'm James. Nice to meet you." I shook the other brothah's hand. "And you are?"

"Francis Miller."

I was scooping this niggah.

"Nice name."

We stared at each other for a brief moment, Barry White singing over the store speakers. 'My darling I, can't get enough of your love, baby.' Aw, Naw, Baby. Now I heard about the DL lifestyle. But I wasn't gay, I have never been raped or anything. I didn't believe you were born with it. Maybe it's Maybelline, who knew?

I never bashed people for what they did and how they did it. I never felt uncomfortable when homosexuals came around me. In fact, I found it questionable when grown men who professed to being men started bashing gays or always brought something remotely gay up in conversation like hearing what others had to say validated their existence.

Like my Pops taught me, "Son when a grown man asks are you gay, inquires about it from your friends or always wants to know what another man is doing with his dick then, Son, he is questioning it for a reason. Because he's a) gay himself and trying to keep the spotlight off the theatre production that goes on behind closed doors and in private inside his room or b) he is interested in you and wants to know the "T," gays call it, before he approaches you."

Daddy was right. I loved and respected all people. That's the way I was raised. But what baffled me was the fact that all sorts of electricity shot through me with the force of a Tech 9 while I stood in this crowded, too noisy store.

Looking at Lloyd.

He was secretly studying me; in his eyes was an untold story I couldn't pen because I didn't know his life or where he came from. Damn, where did I know him from?

I had to close my eyes and suppress it. I was attracted to ole boy with the freckles and I had visions of eating him out the way I did the ladies, since I was an Oral Man with Tongue Lashing Skills.

Lloyd was licking his lips, holding a shirt up to his fabulous chest and he spewed, "Does this look good on me, dawg?"

I loved the way he rocked those Timberland boots. Laced, thank God. If I saw another pair of unlaced boots I was going to scream. His watch glittered. Had to have cost out the ass.

"Yea," I said. "It looks nice on you. You should try those light blue and red jeans over there on the fifth rack from the front. That would look hot. Bitches would be crawling all over you."

Francis smiled, rubbing his chin. He looked like a young Al Pacino if he was Black. Scarface posture, gestures and attitude. I loved it. A little thug niggah. I hated using the "Niggah" word but let's be real, I sometimes used it absent-mindedly.

"And when can I crawl all over you?" he asked, rubbing the fabric of my robe/coat. "Damn, the texture of this get-up is hot, dawg." He looked past me and said, "Let's be real. You're fine, boy. I'm Vers, what are you?"

"You're what?" I asked, confused. "Vers, what the fuck..."

"Versatile."

I was still lost okay with the tunnel vision conversation. "I have never fucked around so what does that mean?"

I was so uncomfortable right now I wanted to croak.

"OK, Top means you do the fucking, Pimp. Bottom means you're the bitch. Vers or Versatile means you take dick and give dick. A Fem you just flamed broiled like burgers and a drag queen you know the drill. So I'm Vers."

"I'm James. I don't know about all this shit." I was getting angry. "I'm not with the program, dawg. You're trying me."

"Naw, dawg. What're you getting mad about? Because I turn you on?"

I frowned. "You're a cocky bitch."

He grinned. "I know. I want you."

"I don't want you."

"Yes you do." He looked in my eyes and I damn near crawled through his because I was on fire, my dick was hot and my ass was an inferno.

"No. I. Don't."

He touched my dick and I melted.

"Like I said, yes you do. Gimme that pussy, dawg. Let me be the first to pop that shit, mah niggah and stop frontin'."

Lloyd walked past me to get the jeans and he paused behind me, letting his huge dick rest on my ass for about three seconds.

"Sorry," he said, apologizing. "Damn, Mama will be mad you don't buy Daddy that sweater," he said, blowing smoke up everyone's asses, making them think we were blood. It worked. He then leaned up to my ear and said, "Can I taste that dick? Come on, dawg. I want them nuts dribbling on my chin so I can blow my whistle and call a technical foul."

I saw myself sticking Grade A dick all in his ass while pulling his hair, making the ass jiggle on the pole. He looked in my eyes and I looked into his. I was nailed to the floor. Neither one of us said anything. I wanted to run and die.

Why did God pick this particular moment in my life to make my body wanna be curious about the bisexual scene?

Why was I feeling this way? My dick was getting hard and I had to take a pair of pants from the rack and model them in front of me so they didn't notice.

Evading his lewd comments I said, "I made the robe/coat."

I lied.

"You did?" asked Francis in shock. "Shit, make me one."

He was beaming.

"Damn that's hot, Son."

Lloyd said, "I'm 'bout to try these pants on. In the back. Dressing Room 3. Be there."

I looked at him and said, "Naw I'm cool, but go try on the pants and let me see how you work that shit, dawg."

He walked to the back, passing by a few females, stopping to throw some game. They smiled when he spoke; a few of them gently touched his arm. He was a rose growing with the daisies. Very smooth. Like how he gave everyone direct eye contact when he spoke to them. He had a big ass. My God. Ass, ass, ASS!

I looked at Francis and said, "I'll be right back."

He grabbed my dick at an angle no one saw but us two and said, "Knock the dust off that ass, he hasn't had any dick in about eight months."

"Why not?"

And he told me why.

Lloyd was in the dressing room, looking himself over in the ceiling-to-floor mirror. Ole boy, James, was right. The jeans were hot with the shirt. He lifted the bottom of the shirt exposing his killer abs. Gave a faint smile, The Rock eyebrow raise. Turned to the side.

The Side Profile was hot.

He wondered why Francis didn't come back there with him. Francis was his first cousin, a man he had always looked up to. He couldn't lie. When he was younger he found his cousin attractive but knowing it was wrong he never put his thoughts to action.

He used to shower with Francis when they were eleven- years-old. They played optimist football together and even then he found that his eyes were little roguish thieves, stealing glances of his magnificent body.

As adults, they hung out together, did everything together from fuck bitches to drinking and partying. They were more like best friends. Francis had been there for him on a number of occasions.

Especially when.

The Car. Screeching. The brakes failed. The boom. The tree. The shattered glass. The explosion. The police. The screams. The...

The door opened and James stared Lloyd deeply in the eyes. Walking inside he closed it, and locked the door.

"I want you to be my first."

Lloyd turned to face him and said, "Damn, niggah I knew you'd come."

"Make me come and shut the fuck up, niggah."

"Damn, aggressive."

"Very aggressive."

James had never felt the urge to pull down another man's pants and fuck the dog shit out of him. Yet he was having those thoughts. What would his father think? His dad had been dead for thirteen years.

"Can I see that ass?"

"Hell yea."

Lloyd turned around, facing the mirror. A rush of lust nearly making him blind, he slowly pulled down his jeans. He wasn't wearing any underwear. James' dick was a brick. Rubbing it, James was licking his lips. Lloyd's ass jiggled.

"Wow, niggah. Goddamn."

He walked up behind him. Started rubbing the hole. It was tight and warm. Lloyd was cooing like a thug niggah and not like a bitch. Definite plus. As a kid James had an infatuation with gangster movies and as a man he had 'em all, from *Scarface* (his favorite) to all the Godfather movies. He nearly came on himself when he saw *American Gangster* last night at the Southland Mall Regal Movie Theatre.

Lloyd turned and gave him some tongue looking deeply into James' eyes. James loved to kiss with his eyes open, too. To see how the other party liked the way his tongue moved. His dick could move even better.

Bitches gave him the nickname the Penetrator because the instant he slid it in he made many women come instantly. It was eleven inches in diameter, three and a half inches thick. Made Castro from the gay movies look like a mere mess.

Lloyd sank to his knees and pulled the Anaconda out.

"Goddamn! That's all you?"

"Hell yea. No dick pumps. All me. My daddy was fourteen inches."

"Fuck, yo!" Lloyd salivated at the mouth and his tonsils were like, "Hell, yea! Do the damn thang!"

He took it into his mouth, slowly sucking on the mushroom head then taking it to the tonsils like a pro. Ole boy swallowed the entire dick whole, making James' eyes bulge out of his head.

"Jesus! Is that all in your throat?"

Lloyd looked up at him, enjoying being throat fucked. James gripped the bushy hair and was banging his hot mouth, the little anal retentive motherfucker.

James had never felt this kind of pleasure from a man, and it was deeper, better and badder. He had stronger jaws, more suction and more passion. The heat made his legs shake. The warmth made him quiver. Lloyd was rubbing his ass.

Pulling the dick out of his mouth he turned James around, spread his ass and began tonguing him slowly, spitting on it, spreading it further, putting in the tips of his index fingers to give it more depth and he tongue fucked him. James, holding on the wall, was stroking his dick, making it harder.

"Oh, yea baby," James said. "Oh yea. Damn. Eat that shit, dawg. Mmm. Shit. Hot. Damn, yo."

His hips were twitching, his ass twirling on Lloyd's tongue. Lloyd's knees were hurting but he didn't care. He ran his tongue all over the hole, savoring the smell. Hints of Gucci cologne filled his nose. James always properly showered, ate a lot of fiber and salads and took care of his body. James had one of the cleanest dicks and asses in the country. He could wear white underwear and it never told his business because he didn't' have any to tell.

James spun on his heels, took Lloyd by the hair and yanked him to his feet, pushing him back against the wall. "Gimme that booty, niggah. Now."

"Damn, dawg..."

Lloyd was about to break. He hadn't been touched in a long time.

James gave him some tongue and said, "Take the Magnum from my pocket and put it on me. I want to watch the Ho in you take care of my dirty work," and James smiled when Lloyd got right to it, not wasting any time.

Once it was on, James bent Lloyd down to touch his toes, and he slowly put his dick deep inside Lloyd. The pleasure and the pain made Lloyd moan.

"Damn, boy. You got a big ass dick."

"Take that shit thug boy and shut the fuck up."

James tapped the ass from the back, making those cheeks jiggle. Lloyd started to cry, the dick was too much, too pleasurable, too goddamn good.

James was tagging it, long stroking it, leaning back and watching the tight hole slide up and down on his pole. He nearly came instantly.

Lloyd stood up, reaching back and holding James' head, throwing the ass back against the pelvis. "Give it all to me."

James was grinning, looking in the mirror.

Lloyd closed his eyes.

BOOM.

The car crash. The tree. His four-year-old son flying into the windshield. No seat belt. Lloyd jumped out of the car bleeding to death. His son was twitching on the glass.

Lloyd was speeding. Try'na look at a niggah driving a Cadillac Escalade. Got distracted. Didn't see the eighteen wheeler. He tried beating his son out of the glass. Nearby residents pulled Lloyd kicking and screaming from the car. Before the paramedics could save his son, when they were running up to the car, the car did the unthinkable:

EXPLODED.

The blast shook the earth and knocked everyone to the ground. Glass sheering into his neck and left arm, as well as injuring near-by witnesses, Lloyd fought everyone. Fists into different faces. His world was over, he wanted to die! Devastated, he could barely see the images before him. Vision failed him miserably. Savagely, he ran at the car and tried to throw himself into the flames. MY SON MY SON OH MY GOD MY SON HELP ME GOD GODDDD HELLLP ME GODDAMN YOU WHY YOU TOOK MY...

Lloyd pushed James off him and started punching at him, the beast exploding. He hurt for his son. He felt like he had failed his own child. The thought of looking his son's mother in the face and saying, "The truck was speeding and it killed my son," was a lie he had to live with. Day and night. Night and Day. James, already made aware of the situation by Francis, took him and held him tightly. He didn't know why but he gave Lloyd his heart at that moment. Sometimes a complete stranger was all one needed. Someone unattached emotionally and physically from your life to give you insight and perspective.

Snot ran from his nose; Lloyd couldn't breathe.

"God took my son. He took my boy."

His pleading eyes bore into James. James saw his soul reaching out for him.

"I was looking at some niggah driving, I was turned on by him, I wanted him and I wasn't watching the road. Catching up to ole boy was more important, at the time, then my son and the fact that his seat belt wasn't on. And out of nowhere, after I made a wrong turn, an eighteen wheeler slammed into my car, sending it careening towards a tree and my son was twitching on the glass and the car exploded before...oh God!"

James held Lloyd tightly, kissing his face. Lloyd hadn't touched another man in months, because this ate him alive. He forced himself to hate men and hate himself. He blamed others for months for his bad decision that cost his son's life, but after therapy he realized he could blame no one but himself. The constant police interrogation. Dealing with family. The lies he told. He vowed to one day find the man that took his attention from the wheel.

"Who was the man you were staring at on that day, Lloyd? Who was he?"

Lloyd looked deep into his eyes, sadly.

"The man was you."

The Beauty Salon

This was a different kind of story. I am pretty sure you're probably thinking, "Yeah, this is about some kinky shit poppin' off in a Salon!" Yea? Am I *right*? Well, *no*. Sorry to burst your bubble. It's not about that.

My magnificent wife was a beautician. She has been doing hair for ten years, plus. She was a gorgeous woman. Or if you let my mama tell it, she had conventional beauty. Yet she had a bubbly personality and that made her smoking hot. She loved cooking for her man and she treated me like a King. She loved people. She looked up to Comedian Monique and she was a big girl.

Doing hair was her passion and was what she lived for. She's been responsible for all those Frankenstein *IT'S ALIVE!* females walking around looking like Hollywood Queens on legs.

They had enough "umph" in their hairstyles to create some Oscar Award buzz. Yet she doesn't have time to please herself because she's always doing hair.

Being her faithful and loving husband, I always called her on it. I told her she should start looking out for herself but she said I was being selfish and that would make *her* look selfish. I thought it was bullshit. She had a heart of gold and I never wanted to change that in my wife. It brought out the best in me. And when the best was brought out everything around me seemed to pulsate with life.

Growing up she was always teased in school for being overweight. This saddened me when she first opened up to me. I remember I had to move hell and heaven to get her to be open about her past. It was very painful for her and there have been plenty of times when I had to hold her and let her cry on my shoulder. It tore me apart watching my woman cry. I don't care how macho you are, when your woman's soul cried you shed tears too.

Having a gorgeous face didn't deter the haters from making her life hell. She said her tits felt like heavy book bags. She didn't know how to fit in because even the ugly kids called her names. There were times she was suicidal and the *only* reason why she never went through with it was because her mother and *God* had never given up on her.

When she was in the fifth grade things took a turn for the worse. It was her birthday and her classmates got together and bought her a present. She felt so good receiving it, the teacher clapping with joy. In fact she showed me photographs from the Big Day, courtesy of her teacher.

"See, I told you they'd come around and show you love" her teacher said, gushing with zeal.

My wife was so happy.

When she ripped off the Winnie-the-Pooh wrapping paper and opened the box the class laughed when she pulled out Twinkie after Twinkie, Lil' Debbie Snack Cakes and a baby doll with an oversized dress and no hair…"

The teacher had every student suspended for ten days.

But my wife was a fighter. I didn't typically like big girls. I loved the chicks with big asses, deep pussies, big titties, little waists and an attitude. However, when I met her when she was in the twelfth grade, I knew I was in love. I couldn't take my eyes off her. I was fucking women left and right. Pussy was my thing, more than my school work – despite making good grades. By then she had several friends, a couple of them being the few who bought her Twinkies back in elementary school. I guess they learned to let bygones be bygones.

Initially, when I started to talk to her I found that she was very attractive and not at all like the other bitches. In fact, she was a Queen. She wouldn't give me the time of day. She thought I was going to play her for a fool. I hated working so hard to win over a woman's attention. Normally, if a bitch blew me off I would call her outlandish names and be done with it. But with her I couldn't do it.

"You're the star basketball player," she told me with a tone you used on a bum. "… "And all these bitches claimed you fucked them. What, the fat girls are next since you boned all the slutty skinny bitches?"

I loved her fire. I loved her attitude. She had the best hairstyle in school. And I was tongue-tied.

"*Damn*, Ma. I just wanna know your name?"

And that opened the door. She stared at me for a long moment before she formally introduced herself and extended her hand. I kissed it, cupping it like a wounded bird. We were inseparable. She started doing hair to make the other girls like her and it worked. She cashed in over four grand alone for the prom. She did everybody's hair in the school. Even a few of the teachers walked around sporting her signature do's.

Now we're happily married and I LOVE IT LOVE IT LOVE IT! I wouldn't have it any other way. She fulfilled me mentally and psychically, in ways other women *never* had. She was my soul mate. She made me want to better myself. I married her because she loved me for me and accepted me for who I was. She tolerated my flaws.

When I left high school I'd done some dumb shit fumbling around with drugs and money laundering and I went to prison. Unwillingly, I did four years and when I got out and I tried to make something of myself. She had been right there by my side and she visited me, sent me money, and nurtured me from behind the walls so I didn't have the urge to fuck dudes in there like all the other guys were doing. I couldn't lie, there were times when I was attracted to a guy in there but I used to pray about it and talk to God.

My flesh was tempted and I was so used to making love to a physical body that I went through withdrawal being in there. I asked God to take away the urges and he did. I happily jacked my dick and kept my soul focused on my lady.

When I tried to push her away, because doing time wasn't easy, she refused to leave. When I called her collect and cursed her for being there for me, because most of my family hadn't visited me or written me a letter, she made sure I was showered with more love and devotion. She read the Bible to me over the phone. She told me Jesus loves me and he loves *us*. She told me she didn't give up the panties to other dudes. She didn't even go to clubs or put herself in temptation's way. She bought a dildo and she'd fuck herself with me on the phone and I'd rub my dick, sitting in the telephone booth with my coat over my lap. That made me so happy, experiencing that little piece of heaven. Hearing my girl come gave me hope and kept me sane.

I owned my own mechanic shop now. It was hard getting it, considering I was an ex-con but my lady kept me grounded.

She paid for my certifications and she drove me to Robert Morgan in South Miami Heights every single day. Even when I didn't want to go she cursed my ass out and pulled me out the door. Retaliating, because I hate being forced or pressured, I'd curse her and call her names and I even called myself leaving her but she never gave up on me because she *knew* and understood that I was trying to push her away because I couldn't believe someone actually cared that much about me.

In the beginning, when everything slowly came together and I graduated from Robert Morgan and enrolled at F.I.U. majoring in business, Satan made it blow up in my face a few months later.

I was kicked out of school when a couple females I met at a party told the police I kept grabbing their asses and I was jailed again. They tried to give me a sex beef and I wasn't having it. If I didn't do something I'd fight hell for just an ounce of heaven. I knew the accusations were lies because I didn't really say three words to them at the party because I was so wrapped up in my wife the entire time. I guess those types of females were used to male interactions and hated the fact that I rejected them. Plus they had flat asses anyways so it'd be more like I was grabbing the table hunting for my keys. Luckily, because of my wife's testimony, and a few loyal friends, I was reinstated back in college and my wife pressed charges on the girls and they wound up doing community service and were kicked out of college.

Now my business was booming, kept us happy and our bills paid. I didn't have a job or a car when I first got home.

Life as an ex-con was hard, and it was even harder finding gainful employment. But my wife came along and put me on my feet and she continued to keep me on my toes. She believed in God with everything in her spirit. She worked with me and taught me patience. She didn't bad mouth me or step on my manhood. She didn't tell our business. She trusted her girlfriends. They came over even when she wasn't there and she knew I'd never cheat on her and I hadn't and never thought about it. If her friends crossed the line I always told her with her friends present. She appreciated my honesty.

She didn't try to change me, like most women tried to do. She accepted me for smoking my weed and drinking my liquor. She knew I loved sometimes, every blue moon, partying with the boys, but one thing she said changed me and I modified the relationship I had with so-called friends.

"Baby, when you were locked up did they visit you, send you money or look after your four- year-old son like I did, even though the child is from another woman?"

Well, no.

"Then you don't need them as friends. They only talk to you because you have a little money. You now own your own shop. You know who your true friends are, which is about two out of the nine you kick it with…"

That in itself made me wanna change.

She could start and finish my sentences. When she shopped at the store she knew how I liked my steamed fish, what size briefs I wore, what colors I would never wear, my shoe and dick sizes and how to carry herself, since she was a reflection of me.

I didn't smoke or curse around her and she had enough joy in her spirit to keep me from hanging out with the boys.

In fact I rarely saw them, but from time to time I did make time *for* them.

You couldn't forget your *true* friends and my woman sometimes invited them over for dinner and they seemed to love it. Believe me, when my wife traveled alone they had her back and would call me if anybody disrespected her. Now it was time to put all the history behind me because I wanted to focus on my wife.

Time to open up shop.

I didn't wonder where the good pussy was because it was right in front of my face. She smiled, lying in the bed we shared for years. The sheets smelled like a week's worth of orgasms. We loved sleeping on them – it intensified our lust. Sometimes I could kiss my hand and I could still taste hints of her pussy.

I was clad in her panty hose. I wanted to do something different. I ripped a huge hole in the front of them to reveal the crotchless panties. I was content with my manhood. She anticipated my touch but I didn't give it to her. I took my time, made her yearn for my love. She started to quiver but I still didn't deliver. I got between her legs and blew my breath on her pussy and she got wetter.

"Oh, baby…Taste it…"

I looked deeply into her eyes.

"No."

She grabbed her titties and I reached up and threw her hands off them.

"Don't make a move unless I approve it."

"Yes, baby."

I leaned on the back of my feet, my nipples erect. "Welcome to the grand opening of my salon!"

"Baby, does it have a name?" she asked. I reached over and grabbed the bottle of Moet. It was still chilled. I popped the cork and picked up a small flute glass. I inserted my index finger in her pussy and I slowly grinded in her until it was wet. She tried to grab her tits again and I gave her a knowing look and her hands retreated to the pillow. She was bumping her pelvis against my hand.

I was cool now. I pulled it out and wiped the inside of the glass with her pussy. I then poured the drink and handed it to her. She had to sit up a little and lean against the headboard. She smelled her pussy then she tried to sip the drink.

"Wait, baby…We are gonna make a toast. Then I'll tell you the name of my salon."

In her eyes read I WANNA FUCK YOU NOW!

I slowly stroked my dick until I started to precum. I was the Precum King. Blow on my neck and precum would come out of nowhere. I reached up and wiped it on her tongue. She sucked my finger, since it was the same one I fingered her with. Smacking her lips she said, "That tastes good."

I took some more precum and wiped it on the inside of my glass. I poured the drink all the way to the top, because I was greedy for wine, and I raised my glass to hers. They clinked.

"To our love," I said, sounding dumb as hell. But fuck it I was a man in love.

"To our love."

We sipped it. Tasted good. Hell, it was spiked with pussy and precum.

"The name of my establishment is the STTTP Salon!"

She killed the drink, licking her lips. She set the glass down. "Ooooh, acronyms! I love it! What does that mean?"

I leaned over her and gave her some tongue – for just a second.

"The Stick Tongue Through The Pus-salon!"

"That's hot, baby! Can I be the secretary?"

"No. You're in my bed. I don't have chairs. And the only hair dryer I have is my breath."

I got between her legs and kissed her pussy. A peck. Then I kissed it again. Her pussy and I had a special relationship. I could make it feel like a twat, cunt, snatch, vagina, coochie and pussy in just ten minutes. She grabbed my head and I pushed her hands off. This killed her because her hands were metal and my body was a huge magnet.

I stuck my tongue so deep inside her she wailed like a spoiled child. I was roaming, imaging my tongue was an archeologist who wanted to find the Valley of the Kings.

I was slurping, using my teeth to softly pull the clit. She shuddered under my touch. I rarely used my fingers, even though she loved when I did. Niggahs who didn't have the proper skills needed dildos, balls, whistles, whips, chains, and fingers to divert the attention away from their ineptness. My lips were my fingers.

My long tongue simply does what it does.

I sometimes ate her pussy for the hell of it. I love her scent, the way she moves to her own groove. I never wanted head in return when I ate my wife. I did it more for me, and watching her come brought me the greatest satisfaction.

I loved the smell on my thick lips. I pushed the hood back so I could see the clit glistening from the bedroom lights. She had a lot of pubic hair, and it needed to be styled so I sat up, leaned over to the nightstand and picked up the small jar of Jell-o pudding. I wiped chocolate all over her pussy hairs and slid some up in her twat. I fingered her, using my right hand to trail my fingertips from her arms, down her breasts and stopped at her navel. This drove her wild.

I was inches from her ear, stroking her pussy.

"You want this dick?"

"Yes, Daddy," she said, barely above a breathy whisper.

I looked at her more fixedly.

"Say you want it."

"I want it."

She doesn't want it yet. "Beg for it."

"I want it, I want it, and I want it."

I licked her earlobe and she rubbed her clit as fast as she could. She was about to die. Her thighs shook and her eyes narrowed.

She is so beautiful! "Say you want this dick."

Tears fell down her face.

"You're torturing me…"

Not enough, my love. Not enough! "SAY YOU WANT THIS DICK!" I screamed in her face.

And she, wide-eyed, said, "I WANT THAT DICK, BABY!"

I sat up and looked down.

"That chocolate is like the cream you use to get a perm. Those pussy hairs have split ends."

I pulled out a pair of scissors from the nightstand drawer and I put them in front of her pussy, careful not to cut my wife. I snipped just a few and she was watching me, smiling.

I have a confession to make. I came up with the Salon, not only because she never made time for herself, but because I got tired of choking on her hairballs in my throat. I hated that with a passion. I didn't know which one I hated most: fish bones or pussy hairs. Imagine talking to a customer and the customer tells you, "Sir, you have a small little hair between your teeth."

And he knew what it was. Very embarrassing. I didn't have the heart to tell her this because when I criticized her or sometimes made suggestions about her body she automatically thought she did something wrong. So I had to come up with an effective way to make those hairs less oblivious to my throat and teeth.

I held up a small pink razor.

"Want me to shave your hair?"

She said, "No. I have black woman's hair. Not Barbie's."

"Should I trim it down?"

"No."

I did it anyway, slowly shaving the hair from her panty line, making it smooth. She smiled, anyway. I was getting rid of a problem that could have caused an argument if I would have told her the truth. So technically I didn't lie to my wife.

She said something anyway.

"Do I tell you how to keep your dick?"

I smiled. "No."

She narrowed her eyes again, the way I loved.

"Then why are you shaving my hair?"

"Because I'm your husband. And what I say goes."

"Shit, you got it like that, huh?"

"Hell, yeah."

"Well on this pussy board it's stalemate, because I don't like being shaved. So hurry up before I change my mind."

"Ok."

I put the razor down and got out of the bed. I picked up my jeans and put them on. She was confused, shaking her head.

"Where are you going?"

"Stalemate, remember? If I can't do what I want then you can't get what you want. I changed my mind about giving you this good dick. Damn, it's big and hard, too. What a waste of a hard on…"

I zipped them up, thinking about what I was going to do. I could go to the office and look over the account receipts. Yea I could do that. Less work I would have to do tomorrow.

She jumped out of the bed and snatched me by the jeans.

"You are going to give me this dick."

I faked a yawn.

"No. I'm tired. I got a headache."

She pushed me on the bed and tried to unbuckle my pants. This was hot. She was trying to force them off. Damn she couldn't control herself.

I pushed her hands off me and she grabbed them again, determined to get the beef steak. She unbuckled them and zipped them down.

"GIVE ME THIS DICK, NIGGAH!"

Like a beast she pulled my pants down, taking my dick into her mouth. Well I never! She sucked me with a sense of urgency I had never seen before. Damn, this turned me on. She wanted me so bad she would rape a niggah? RAPE ME BABY, HELL YEA. Take this dick from Daddy. Work for that shit. I was captivated, getting lost in the warmth. She kept spitting on it, and jacking it. She knew just what I liked. I loved every minute of it.

She made me feel like the luckiest man alive.

She hit all the right spots because I had to come. But as good as it felt it was still too early. I sat up and took her by the hair.

"I'm not done with your perm yet."

I pushed her big ass on her back and spread her legs. The chocolate pudding smeared on her thighs. My cum went back into my testicles. I could feel it.

I then said, "OK, time to rinse the chocolate perm off. And put the pussy under the blow dryer."

I began to eat again, slurping on the pussy, using my fingers -- even though I didn't want to. She loved every minute of it. I could see the buildup in her eyes. She was a pressure pipe and she was about to explode. I loved the way she gripped the sheets and bit her bottom lip. She was fucking my tongue in ways she never fucked my dick. Her eyes rolled to the back of her head.

"I'm about to come…"

No, no. Not yet, big girl. I stopped cold turkey.

"No, not yet. It's too soon."

She whined. "But baby!"

"Trust me. Prolonging your orgasm will make it ten times stronger."

She started to cry. Seriously. She loved to come so much she had become addicted to it. And I wasn't giving her what she wanted tonight. Sometimes you had to keep your wife contained and let her know it's not all about penetration and coming. It's about the love. The mental stimulation. The eagerness. I didn't want her to cry, though. It tore me to pieces when I saw her tears. But she had to learn self-control and patience.

I stared at her for about five minutes, saying nothing.

She hated the silence. She pouted.

"Baby…why are you so quiet?"

I picked my nails, ignoring her.

She hated to be ignored.

"BABY?"

As if she was a stranger, I asked, "I'm sorry, do I know you?"

Through clenched teeth she said, "Baby fuck me."

"Your hair isn't dry yet. You have to wait until the style is finished."

She got an attitude. She cut her eyes at me viciously. She pointed at me.

"Fuck the hairstyle – I want some dick."

I shook my head.

"No."

I slapped her hand out of my face. I was Daddy, Obey my rules.

She lay on her back and closed her eyes. I started to massage her, deeply getting into her skin. I was rubbing her thighs…her arms.

I trailed my fingers to her tits.

"Remember when I told you to put yourself first and stop doing things for other people all the time?"

She was trembling.

"Yes."

I sucked the pussy, the sound filling my ears and making me smile.

She had to come again. I stood up and said, "I love you. Good night. I'm going to bed now."

"You motherfucker! I wanna come."

"No, baby."

"I'm going to finish it myself."

I poured the Moet all over her and she got mad. "Cool off, baby. Learn patience."

"I don't want patience. I wanna be fucked."

"Why are you so needy?" I asked, wanting to laugh. I loved driving her crazy.

"You're my husband…there's no such thing as being needy."

"We don't always get what we want."

"Oh my God! Just put it in me and fuck me until I can't move."

"No."

I kissed her forehead and she tried to slap me.

"I love you. I'll sleep on the couch. Ciao."

I grabbed my pillow and sat on the couch. Sometimes you had to put yourself first.

And I did just that.

With a smile on my face I wrapped the covers around me and I closed my eyes and prayed.

Listening to her boisterous obscenities, I was falling asleep.

I just wanted to shave her pussy anyways. And that mission was complete.

What Goes Around

DOWN SOUTH, PERRINE, FLORIDA.
POINT ROYALE SHOPPING PLAZA.

Goddamn my foot was sore.

I was 6 feet 5, 205 pounds with 4 percent body fat. I had a low fade, was a bisexual male but it was carefully, cautiously hidden from the human naked eye. I had on a dirty white wife beater and a construction vest that was too small because my boss gave out the XXL vest to a new hire who couldn't paint stripes on Florida's roads to save his life. Plus the Niggah tried to tell me what to do.

Telling me the ropes of a job he'd been on for an hour when I had graduated to swinging from vine to vine like Tarzan before he got there. He was not on my level.

I have been working since 6 a.m. Worked in the flaming sun for twelve hours straight. I was a certified paint striper. I was responsible for motherfuckers staying in their lanes when driving on the road. I painted the turning arrows, measured the shit – all that. And I was only 27-years-old.

And thinking about my boss, Bernie Symbols (The Preacher's Son), a 200-pound, ex-wrestler from Daytona Beach, Florida, I got even more pissed. He tried to embarrass me today on the job by telling all the fellahs that he fucked my ex-girlfriend that she sucked his dick and she swallowed his nut. I laughed, too, and he got thrown off when I reciprocated the gesture by telling the fellahs that I fucked his mama. I fucked that old bitch in the ass, too. He thought I was playing. Yea, right Niggah. I didn't lie on my dick.

My panties were sweaty and gripped my ass like a second skin. I had long, thick dreads that would put Bob Marley to shame. I loved my hair. I always had a fascination with them. Maintaining their cleanliness was a bitch. Looking in the rear view mirror of my supped-up purple Chevy with Janet Jackson's 1993 *Rolling Stone* magazine cover airbrushed on the trunk, I really didn't feel like being out in the world. I kept thinking about popping a few honeys on the way home and probably getting one to eat my ass while I jacked my dick, pretending she was 1963's Eartha Kitt.

When I parked my Chevy in the handicapped spot of the parking lot at the local electronic store, I pulled once more on my joint and held the smoke in my lungs, my eyes watering. This was that Louisiana Kush shit right here. My boy, Jack (with his fat, afro-wearing ass) always hooked me up with this shit. I didn't have the proper handicapped tag to park here but who gave a damn about rules?

I was a man who loved panties so much I wore them and never told a soul. I was a man who loved women's underwear so much I wrote short stories about them, what I would do to them. I would fuck a good pair of panties before I fucked a bitch, truth be told. I'm being real about this shit right now.

As a dedicated construction worker, life in the streets could be hell on earth and sometimes I thought one of those chicks from my past must have put roots on me because I couldn't nurture a respectable relationship with another female to save my life, lights or house payments. On the roads with a blaring sun beating down on you, there was never any cold water and the owner of the road construction company, Pastor Lenny, didn't care if we farted or fainted. I had to pant like a dying whale before he offered me anything, which was never enough to wet my throat. And the public didn't respect us. Between the ex-cons (who were hard-working individuals) flirting with the flowing skirts that pranced by on the sidewalks of Liberty City, Florida and disrespectful motorists who ignored every request to SLOW up while coming through our work area, I wanted to barf. I definitely didn't want to do this line of work for the rest of my life. I was getting older and things were changing about me so I knew that I had to get with the program.

I was initially wearing boxers under my clothes at work. But that quickly gave me a rash on my testicles after all the sweat soaked into my skin so wearing a thin pair of panties were both easier on my bulging cock and lighter on my ass. I loved the feel of silk on my torso when I leaned over in commuter traffic managing the Paint Striper.

Pushing that out of my freaky brain, I tried to stop thinking about work. I needed to park somewhere else but I decided to stay in the handicapped spot. I wasn't authorized to park there but there were no parking spots available. I looked around for 5-0. I had to always be on alert for the cops, especially driving an expensive high-performance car like mine. I had Spreewell rims spinning on the tires. I shelled out $6,000 for them. My Booming System LL Cool J would hate on. The tinted windows allowed me to get my dick sucked in peace. Rene Elizondo covering Janet's tits on the trunk was the product of admiration throughout the 'hood. I won thirty car competitions with Janet. She's my bitch!

My right foot ached like freaking hell when I started walking, damn near limping, to the entrance of the store. Part of me wanted to go home. I had to cook, clean up my place, call some bitches over, but I decided against that.

My foot was giving me hell, so all the feelings were diverted from my dick.

I couldn't afford the $200 fine if the police caught me parking there but oh, well. I had to get in and get out as quickly as possible. I hated shopping with a passion.

I wasn't one to follow the rules all the freaking time.

A chubby bitch ran over my foot today when I was at work. All those flashy safety cones directing traffic wasn't enough for her stupid, non-driving ass! Plus she was a Cuban and they never followed the rules of the road. I was going to let it slide but she said, "You need to watch what the hell your black ass is doing…"

I slowly looked at her, gritting my teeth.

"Excuse me?"

My boy Don stopped using the Grind machine, looking over at us, caked with dirt. Leonard was shaking his head, laughing, with tree bark chips in his hair.

"You heard me! You guys have been working on this road for seven months and I'm getting tired of slowing up just to come through here."

My foot was killing me. I hope she didn't break anything.

I said, "Go to hell, bitch."

"Fuck you, Niggah!"

"Niggah? I don't tolerate your fat Cuban ass calling me out my name."

"Well…"

"Stay right here!"

I was screaming, my voice booming past the oak trees. Leonard stood in front of me and Don told the woman she should wait for the police so I could file charges.

"I don't wait for no police!"

"Get this bitch outta here!" I spewed, wanting to wrap my hands around her sweaty throat and choke the life out of her.

"You go to hell, Mister!"

Does she have a life? Why is she arguing with me? Bitch press your foot on the pedal and leave me alone! "I should get my man to beat your ass."

"Ha! Your man who?"

I shot my cuffs.

"His name is Fidel Castro, Ho! Wait right there while I call him. I got his number on speed dial."

"Fuck you!"

And she cursed me out in Spanish, speeding off and my boys were laughing but my foot wasn't laughing at all. The "Little Piggy" of my toes wouldn't be going to the market, staying home nor having roast beef anytime soon.

I was drained. On the way here I stopped by Tianna's house, some freaky bitch I met at the Indoor Flea Market in this very same shopping plaza three months but never got around to hooking up with her Asian/Black ass because of my crazy work schedule. And even though pussy was all good, and *new* pussy was even better, pussy alone and coming inside a bitch wasn't going to pay my bills. If anything the bitch would wind up pregnant and that's one bill I was afraid of – child support.

Anyways. Tianna was sexy, sensual, and she gave me the best phone sex of my life. She was 5 feet 4, which I loved because I was so damn tall, and I loved petite Hoes. To a small bitch like that my nine-inch, cut dick looked twelve inches. She sucked my dirty dick expertly, sucked twelve hours of work right off me like it was free candy. She loved pulling my dick out of the panties and working her magic. She initially told me she loved the fact that I could be in tune with my feminine side. That made her pussy wet and her clit jealous. Plus, I looked better than her in panties, wasn't that a bitch?

I lay on her couch, dirt all over me, smelling like nuts, ass and a faint rush of Cool Water cologne I sprayed on me before leaving for work this morning after my shower.

She had a framed poster of Billie Holiday and another of Phyllis Hyman on her walls. I loved the neo-soul in this room.

She pulled my sweat pants down to my Timberland boots. Nuts jumping up and down as she worked those lips, 2 Live Crew blasting in the background. "Hood Rat Hoochie Mama" shit, old shit, played out shit that I didn't care to hear. I fucked those pretty lips, watching her toss that long, jet-black hair all over my hips.

"I wanna feel those tonsils, bitch!"

I grabbed the back of her head, making her gag. I loved the way she moaned, like a helpless woman trapped on railroad tracks. My dick was the train.

"Hold your breath, bitch. Suck my muthafuckin' dick, Ho! Suck the nuts, too! I'm not playing with you! Yea, bitch, a Niggah hasn't had any pussy in two months."

And I had two months worth of nut built up in me. I hadn't even jacked off.

"Turn over, Niggah," she convincingly demanded and I did. To my surprise, she ate my ass, driving me crazy. My ass cheeks were all up in her face and that turned me on. I wasn't going to front! She moaned and used that tongue to play in my shit and she didn't care that I didn't shower or that I took a shit before getting to her house, but I cleaned up down there pretty good so I wasn't worried.

I got lost in her tongue action. Her game was tight. I let her lick my asshole like I had a pussy.

I damn near pulled my hair out. That slick tongue went from my hole to the back of my nuts, where she gripped them, pulled my dick back to her, and sucked the swollen head.

Her tongue finding my nuts again, she massaged my chocolate opening…I was about to cry. My legs shook. My toes curled in my boots. Oh, shit, bitch! Shit shit shit!

"Fuck this!"

I couldn't take it anymore. I wanted this bitch.

"Ho, gimme this pussy!" I told her, pure Thug Style.

I stood up, threw the bitch on the sofa and dove in the pussy. I pulled her panties to the side, drenched with vaginal fluid, and ate her right there.

My panties-clad ass in the air, I licked both her enticing holes, pushed those legs back, and tongued her dripping twat like she was Lil' Kim saying she didn't want dick tonight.

She said something in Asian. I fingered her pussy, making her suck the juices off my fingers. I then burst open and just fell in the pussy, my nine-inch dick sliding in like role call.

I beat the pussy up, giving it to her raw dog. A Niggah was so horny I didn't give a fuck about AIDS or other STDs. Plus she had the cleanest pussy known to man and this kind of pussy a man deserved to experience without the aid of plastic.

Niggah, are you crazy! Why didn't you wear a Jimmy? I thought to myself, dismissing the thought when I looked at my ass wiggling in the mirror in these panties.

I stared at the picture of her boyfriend on the entertainment shelf as her tightness gripped my dick like clouds on air. I imagined it was him fucking me like I was fucking his tramp. Niggah was sexy, fine as fuck.

I pushed her legs back (even with her ears) and home girl moaned so loud, calling me daddy.

"Baby stick it in my ass please, daddy!"

I did just that, sucked on that asshole to lube it up, slid my dick in there, I know that shit hurt, and fucked her 'til I came.

When I did, I pulled out, watching her do a damn somersault to the doggy position and she caught all my nut on her tongue.

"Clean my dick, bitch!"

I shoved my dick in her mouth, making her suck the little brown shit off I saw. Wasn't much. Turned me off.

It was shit. I didn't love the Hoe. Snoop Dogg taught me that. My mama always taught me, when you drop shit you clean it up.

"Play with my nut, Ho! Yea, just like dat. Let me see dat shit. Yeah, bitch!"

I grabbed her drenched-with-sweat blouse in a closed fist and pulled her up to me; French kissed her, played with my nut, and used my tongue to push it down her throat, swallowing some of my own.

And then I zipped up, got my keys and got somewhere.

Ж

Escaping the devastatingly hot rays of the unapologetic sun, I was thankful for the shade in the store. Felt really good. I saw a tall, caramel-colored Niggah staring at me from one of the CD racks. I saw him somewhere before, couldn't quite grasp it. He looked like Mekhi Pfeiffer. No bullshit. But better. He actually greeted me when I entered the crowded-to-capacity electronics store. He had a heart-warming smile, all his teeth perfectly white and straight. His yellow uniform shirt with the name AVON B. SEXY on his name tag caught my attention, but I kept walking.

I was there for one reason.

I loved women; I loved watching big titties and Hoes with the big asses waddle by wherever I go. How could I not? But I loved Niggahs, too. I loved chocolate. I wasn't a fan of vanilla chocolate. He had to be dark-skinned and tall because piss-colored Niggahs thought they were the gems of the earth and couldn't suck a dick or take a pipe to save their lives.

Maybe because women treated Niggahs so badly these days I had to actually go give up the ass to see *why* they hated us so much.

Women were always in my face telling me what we did wrong. Half of their asses were on welfare, had WIC coupons in picture frames and cheated everyone out of money on a daily basis, yet they're in my face demeaning me and black men in general because they were dumb enough to spread their legs before getting to know their man. That wasn't my fault.

Take responsibility for your own actions. Learn your audience before carnal play.

A few women who were interested in me blew me off because I didn't want to give up my money, dick or have those nappy-headed demon-influenced kids in my face. I wasn't going to take care of another man's responsibility.

I didn't do Baby Daddy drama.

I didn't have time for it.

With a man, I didn't have to go through that.

We met up, did what we do, and did what we should when it was over.

No drama. No strings.

No attachments.

I still didn't know why, but I was stuck in this on-the-low lifestyle. I tried it and I loved it, and couldn't turn back. I lived my life under the radar. I didn't go to gay clubs and I didn't support anything gay. I kept the lifestyle away from my home. I couldn't afford for any of this to get out to my family.

My green Michael Chivo sweat pants hung under my ass. I had a bubble back there, and Avon's eyes fell on it when I walked past him and headed to the R&B section to buy Keisha Cole's latest album, produced by Krucial Keys and I needed to buy another copy of Janet's *Damita Jo* CD again because my baby niece, Sumatra, age four, accidentally, or purposely, used Janet and my Brandy CD to play in the toilet doing her version of Who Sunk my Battle Ship with my goddamn CDs!

I was already mad because I wasn't getting benefits from my employer. They were a privately owned company, and I knew that upon getting the job. What I didn't know was that I wouldn't be getting a 401 (K), medical and dental. And since people said I looked like WWE wrestler The Rock I needed the shit so I could stay off the chain. I kept myself up.

I felt really shitty. And all sorts of feelings surged through my body.

I searched every CD rack for Keisha Cole. Where was the bitch? I walked past three Niggahs dressed like a Nelly video and paused in front of Luther Vandross, saying a silent prayer for his family.

There was Avon, staring. He had the same eyes that stared back at me from Tianna's house. He was the Niggah on the photo. *Whoa.* Small world. But oh well, Tianna got tagged today. I felt myself getting hot, the sweat slowly vaporizing from my body, thanks to the AC. I looked in his hazel eyes and smiled, asking him, "Where the fuck is Keisha Cole?"

He seemed relieved I didn't sound like some faggot. He was summing me up and getting a feel for me. His eyes bore down on mine, and I could feel the chemistry building. Made my dick hard, and when I looked down at him, his dick was hard, too, and he had a big one. He pulled his shirt out of his pants and the hard on was gone. Goddamn! He nodded towards the Entrance.

"She's up front, I'll show you."

I wanted to flirt.

"Damn, service like that? What did I do to deserve that?"

"You're a hard-working Niggah, judging from those dirty construction clothes! And we are an electronics store; I have to put the customer first. Plus, I accidentally ran over your boot today when you were stripping the roads in North Miami Beach—"

I stared at him in shock. I thought a Cuban woman ran over my foot, but the windows were very tinted so I had no way of knowing if a male or female drove anyway. Lord. I cursed out an innocent woman.

Avon went on.

"I was on my way to work. I was in a rush. Sorry 'bout that, playa."

Heading for the front of the store, I looked at him: he was tall, sexy and had a nice ass. I smiled, and decided to walk on the side of him.

I said," I should sue your ass, running over my foot. I had just painted that damn turning lane line and you ran over it with your Suburban, rushing, and you caught my foot."

He looked at me with a smile. "Get the Keisha Cole CD, and come to my register."

"I gotta get *Damita Jo*, too."

"Go get her, I'll ring you up."

He didn't ring me up; I got two free CD's. On Avon.

I hate to say it but that was four months ago.

Now Avon and I are the best of friends. I guessed he knew I fucked around on the side. I *rarely* fucked around. I had to be high on weed to actually get fucked by another man, but I had serious feelings for him. We confided in each other. He told me a lot about himself, the high school he went to, that he was actually married to some chick. And then one night at Avon's crib, in North Miami Beach, I told him I was bisexual, in the closet, and wasn't with the faggot shit. I didn't do gay clubs, never have and I didn't hook up with them on the Internet.

And he looked at me and drank some of his Hennessy liquor *straight* from the bottle. He unzipped his pants and his dick was on display. He didn't wear any underwear. He then told me to take his pants off and I did, down to his Air Force Ones and I sucked his ten inches right there on his leather sofa. I took my time, going up and down, testing my deep throat skills. Drove his ass wild.

"I wanted you for a while, Niggah," said Avon, drinking from the bottle, Tupac blaring. "Just me and my Bitch." He had red light bulbs in the lamps, I loved the read glow…He then looked at me, set the bottle down, stood up, grabbed me by my Phat Farm shirt, pulled me to his face and he tongued me, slowly.

"I wanna fuck you. I have never been turned on by a Niggah; I never fucked a dude so I'ma little uneasy but you're so fucking fine how could I not give you this Anaconda Snake?"

He had a very deep voice – a cross between Barry White and OJ Simpson.

Pulling my pants down, he bent me over the low table and ate me out right there, pouring liquor on my ass, soaking into my pink panties; I could feel the cold liquid trailing down my body. He sucked it off.

Felt so goddamn good.

"Damn, Niggah. Your ass looks so appealing in these panties. Wow, man. Goddamn, yo! I am going to drill for oil!"

Then he put on a Magnum rubber, finger fucked me, sucking my essence down his throat. Then he slid his condom-clad dick inside me, fucking me so hard, so fast, and so good I came all over my boots.

"I love how your ass jiggles in these pink panties! Damn, this is hot!"

He slapped my ass, putting one foot up on the table. I saw his nuts bouncing off my ass in the mirror behind him. What a sight. I couldn't take it anymore, I was about to pass out.

He pulled out of me, looking like a sensual beast, we both were sweaty, and it was hot in there, and he lay me on the couch, put my legs back and said, "I know this is how you fucked one of my bitches. Her name is Tianna!"

He went up in me and fucked the shit outta me 'til he came and when he did he stood up on the couch, towering over me and he came in my mouth.

He then pulled me up to him, both of us standing on the chair, and he French kissed me, playing with his nut, and pushed it down my throat with his tongue, swallowing some of his own.

Then he grabbed my keys, tossed them to me and pressed play on his VCR. There I was fucking his girl, Tianna, before going to the electronics store.

"She didn't know I filmed her. I had a feeling she was fucking around on me, giving away my pussy. Small twist of fate it was you. She thought she was working me. Nah, Niggah. I installed my camera in her place on the entertainment shelf. So you got back what you gave me, but we cool, we boys. Just call it payback."

And with that he left his house and told me, "Lock up behind yourself when you leave. I gotta go to my second job at Club Twist on South Beach. By the way, you got some good ass, Niggah! And keep the panties. They look good on you."

The door closed behind him. All I could do was stand there, on the couch, feeling dumb, used and stupid.

With a smile on my face.

Obese Booty Call

Wanting to read the new Sistah Souljah novel, *Midnight*, I felt like a blooming rose in the middle of sunlight when I opened my dusty drapes. I was so tired I was about to fall on my face. My only sister Tasha has been going through some trying times and since she didn't have a place to live I let her live with me until she moved in with her children's father. But thinking of my three nieces and two nephews, I grew pensive. My light bill, grocery bill and water bill exploded by sixty percent when they lived with me. Before they came my bill lingered around a hundred for the lights, ninety for the water and when I had to pay over $300 for my lights after my sister moved in I sat her down and had a talk with her – what good that did. She figured since I was big brother she could move in rent free and do what she wanted. No. It didn't work that way. Plus her bad ass kids were nerve-wrecking. I couldn't get an ounce of sleep. My nephew Paul, who was 8-years-old, wanted to pound on the walls while listening to 50 Cent. This angered me. When I did get up and put on a robe, I went into my bathroom to wash my face and I came face-to-face with my 13-year-old niece in my shower with all of my body gel open. She had water all in the cream-colored rugs, the music blaring and she was singing a Whitney Houston cut. I snatched her ass out of my bathroom naked and kicked her ass out of my room. I was too mad. SO I went to my sister and told her the most lovingly memorable thing I had ever told her.

"GET YOUR KIDS AND YOUR SHIT AND GET THE FUCK OUT NOW!"

She said she hated me. Oh, well. I loved her and my nieces and nephews but they had the same Daddy and those demon seeds were his responsibilities not mine. So I didn't lose any sleep.

I started sneezing my ass off. Just the sight of dust sent me into a sinus fit. I was sneezing so badly I couldn't catch my breath. I was eyeing the Benadryl sinus pills but the more I sneezed the weaker I seemed to feel. I couldn't even catch my breath. I had to hold onto the island counter in the kitchen to keep my balance. I needed to dust the shelves, ceiling fan and drapes in my home and buy some of that Febreeze to cleanse the air and the ceiling fan but I've been lazy as of late. Then maybe I wouldn't be sneezing so badly. Nothing was going right in my life. I wasn't a very optimistic person. My Daddy named me Climax Alize because he was drunk off Alize when he came in my mother's pussy. I hated the name. I used to be ashamed of it in school because I was the butt of a thousand jokes.

Fighting horniness, I walked past the low table (cluttered with old VIBE magazines), looking GQ smooth in an expensive Gucci leather jacket, Louis Vuitton penny loafers and a pair of black Coogi slacks.

All around my living room were packed boxes. I neatly packed all of my shit. Against my better judgment I shouldn't have given in so easily when my landlord told me to leave the premises. That threw me for a loop. Eight months ago I lost my apartment in Denver. I was going through a lot. I was jacking my dick with baby-oil-drenched Saran Wrap three times a day, up three percent from previous months. I had to drop out of college because the Department of Education decided to renege on the loans and I didn't have that kind of money to spare. I tried applying for scholarships but that didn't do an ounce of good.

I had to hear it from my parents. I had to tell them where to get off and what part of my ass they could kiss. This was my life and I dictated what went on. If I dropped out of school then get over it.

Moving here to Philadelphia was a Godsend. I had filled out an online job application for a pharmaceuticals company and I had gotten the $19.95 an hour pay slot. But with that came stress and jealous white people who undermined everything I'd ever done.

My cousin, Sea Weed (when he *saw* weed he *smoked* it) lived in Arthur Mays Villas (dubbed Chocolate City) in Goulds, Florida (Miami) and he'd phoned me and asked me to visit. I was reluctant. I really didn't want to go visit him because when we were thirteen we fucked each other in my mama's shower and I didn't care to have a relationship with him. I didn't want to be reminded that he made me wear my mother's wig and bend over and touch my toes in her oversized Granny panties and chipped high heels. Everybody did something in their lives they weren't proud of and I was no exception.

Plus my mother and his mother basically hated each other and my mama could be a looney bitch when she wanted to be. If you took someone's side over hers she believed that to be the ultimate betrayal and I didn't feel like hearing that shit from her so initially I told Sea Weed, I pass.

"But, Cuz! You need to come to the realest part of Miami. Fuck South Beach and all that jazz. I can hook you up with the bitches, lace your weed with some coke and call it a day."

He is so ghetto! "Naw, Cuz," I responded, packing some statuettes in an unmarked box.

"You need to, Man. I know you're not pouting about losing your job."

You have some nerve! "Brothah Man, I am very upset. Do you know what I am losing? I am losing everything I worked so hard for."

"Just pick yourself up and try again."

"Did you say that when your broke ass moved in with your Baby Mama and you were caught fucking her Daddy in the ass?"

"Man, why did you go there?"

"It's not always easy to pick up and move on. I been in Denver for three months and already Satan has turned my life into the Book of fucking Job."

"Man cheer up. Just fly down to Miami, stay with me and get your mind off things. You never experienced Miami. Maybe you can find a job here."

"Yea, if I was bilingual. I heard about high-ass Miami. The cost of living is shit, bruh. Seriously. I like Denver and I don't want to leave. But I have to."

"If you change your mind…"

"I will let you know."

"Well, holla. Niggah…"

"Whatever, Sea Weed."

"Remember, pray about it."

"Pray about it?"

My brows rose.

"Pray? P-R-A-Y?"

"Yes," he said, chuckling. "Pray about it."

"Spell pray."

"P-R-A-Y!"

"Naw, it's N-O-T-Y-O-U. Not you, bruh. You don't even believe in God."

"Bye, Niggah."

I was sitting on the couch, clad in sweaty coveralls. Ashanti's video was on BET and she had soda cans in her hair as hair rollers, sashaying that fat ass, singing about she got that Good-Good. Bitch, I bet you do. I didn't know what to do. Everything was happening so fast. I couldn't think straight. I needed a joint but I was trying to cut back on smoking so much. My doctor said weed killed your brain cells and that shit right there, for some reason, put the fear of God in my heart.

I was pissed off because I had lost my place and I may have to summon my Daddy and move back in with him, which I wasn't looking forward to. When you had your own shit for years and Satan decided to play checkers with your living room furniture you were antsy about moving back in with your parents, following their fucked rules. In my heart I knew I had to do what I had to do but goddamn, living with my Pops…out of the question.

I loved Denver and I loved my job at Felix Pharmaceuticals but I had to hoola hoop through flaming tunnels just to be as good as the white boys and I failed and I was fired for using the word 'Niggah' on my goddamn lunch break. Now with no income and my boss tarnishing my image all over Denver I couldn't get a job anywhere and my apartment has to go so I didn't choke.

The phone broke the tranquility in my bedroom, disturbing me from a deep sleep. Now my dream was fucked up! I was fucking Halle Berry in the ass while Ciara did the One-Two Step all over my nuts. Bitch gave good brain, too. Goddamn

Ring!

Who the hell was that calling me at…I was trying to open my eyes but I was drained and my eyes were lazy sonsofbitches with attitude and they weren't with the program. They didn't feel like being the…look out. I tried to open them but they failed me, the room an absolute blur.

Ring.

I realized the light was still on. And as the room came into focus, I smiled because my Shiatsu was asleep at the foot of the bed.

Ring.

Tiredly reaching over, I picked up the cordless phone.

"Hello…"

"Are you awake?"

"Yea, girl. I was fucking two bitches at the same time but as always you ruined my fantasy."

"Your broke ass can't afford a fantasy."

"I know we're not going to do this right?"

I prided myself on being a gentleman. I was a lover of animals because a Pit Bull lived in my dick and I loved the ladies. Women. Classy Broads. And even the Hoes. As a man you always wanted a variety of things available to set the tone of your day or to pick a woman who fits the mood of your evening. I didn't care if she was obese, sexy, retarded or despondent. A woman was a woman and I loved opening doors for them, buying all the ladies at my job roses every Valentine's Day and pampering them all with a catered dinner right in the office. I loved pulling out their chairs, flirting with them without trying to scratch and sniff the pussy and I loved going out with them to the Grown and Sexy Bar by the Dadeland Mall. All of that had to do with my upbringing. I had a single parent home. My mother, Grace, left my father when I was about 7-years-old. I had a lot of anger and I used to write in journals to channel it. When Mom moved out I hated women, vowing to always despise them. How could Mama divorce Daddy and leave us all alone? Without a woman in the house our home went to hell. Daddy couldn't cook to save his life. He kept mixing the colored clothes with the whites and the whites came out red and the blacks were faded because he poured in too much bleach. I never saw a grown man cry until Dad settled on the couch, his face in his hands. Sadness befell the room like a thick cloud of smoke. The tension stung my eyes. I remember sitting by him, wrapping my arms around my hero. He always maintained gainful employment, but that wasn't enough for Mama. Hot in the ass, she fucked the mailman, wound up pregnant and decided to discover America using her dripping snatch and not her intelligence. Daddy cried until we both fell asleep and when we awakened, he had a talk with me. He told me that I may have convictions about Mama and I may have hate but he told me to love her anyway. He made me promise him that I wouldn't get so wrapped in a woman that I lost my own identity.

"It's important to have your own life outside your wife, son. It's easy to meet and fall in love. It's easy to get caught up in the dynamics of it."

He stood up and walked over to the bar. My eyes followed him. He looked frail and weak and it rubbed off on me.

"A woman comes along and fills the void in your heart and suddenly you think she can outdo God," he said bluntly, pouring himself a stiff drink. "You modify time with your friends, and you don't have time for your boys. You have to remember, your friends were there before she came along."

He wolfed down the drink, smacking his lips.

"Those will be the same friends who let you cry on their shoulder when she leaves. That was my mistake, Son," he went on, facing me, leaning against the corroding bar. "I cut off my friends because she said so. Pussy was so good I would do anything for her and she knew it. Son, never let your woman know her pussy is golden. She will crush you with it. Put on a front. Grab your balls and show her who's boss. Please adhere to what I'm saying. When you meet a lady make sure she isn't a whore. If she makes you feel like you can conquer the world make sure your head isn't in the clouds."

He sat by me. I looked into his eyes.

"Son, never marry the first piece of pussy you get. My father never taught me that. In fact, when it came to pussy my father *was* a pussy. He let his woman run him and run his life and he was quite content with that."

He rubbed my head, trying to hide his grief. I loved the fact that my father had a vulnerable side. It taught me that I could display my emotions without looking like a sissy.

"Learn her, take her out and talk to her. Stay on the phone with her; get on her nerves to secretly find out if she can tolerate you. Ask what her favorite color is and what her favorite song is. Tell her *your* favorites *first* to see if she miraculously says, 'Oh, Barry White is my favorite singer too!' Turn it on and study her without making it obvious. If she doesn't know a word of the song then you know she's a goddamn liar. Send all your male cousins and friends up to her one by one and tell them to try to bed her. If she opens her legs then son don't get angry. She was never yours. Don't fight over a piece of ass. It isn't worth the jail time, grief, stress or sleepless nights. If I see you crying over a bitch I will whip your motherfucking ass, Son."

I shuddered when he said it. He looked me deep in the eyes and grabbed my chin, shaking it.

"I hope you're listening. I hope it's registering in your brain."

"It is, Dad."

"I didn't have anybody to teach me."

"Dad, I won't let you down."

"Don't let *you* down, Son. I'm telling you for your benefit."

"Ok, Dad."

He released my chin.

"…But if she raises hell and brings them to your face and tells you what they were trying to do to her behind your back then son you have a winner."

I took it to heart.

He stood up, feeling good about our talk. I felt good as well. The thought of girls still terrified me. They seemed to be part of a secret society. They were always emotional. He was taking off his belt, then unbuttoning his jacket.

Dad, are you ok?"

There was an inferno in his eyes.

"Yes, I am. I have to make sure my words have sunk in your head."

"They did."

He whipped my ass with the leather belt, shocking me.

He got his point across loud and clear.

My homeboys always dissed me because of my love for women. They had a nickname for me. It was "Jumper Draws." I used to laugh, trying to figure out what the hell that meant. So one day, during a very intense basketball game, I called a time out, my 6 foot, 7 inch frame dripping in sweat and asked Leonard, an IBM exec, "What does Jumper Draws mean, Man?"

Everyone started laughing. A few honeys, chatting on the bleachers, were checking me out. The short Asian blond bombshell kept looking at my dick print behind my drenched gym shorts.

Leonard, a short, stocky dude with a receding hairline, chuckled.

"You know what it means, Michael Johnson. It's when you kiss the girls' asses, spending all your money on them hoping to Jump their Bones."

We slapped palms, but he was off base, I didn't look at women as door mats. I looked at them as true Queens. They were the *Mothers* of the earth, the Bait on the Hook to lure the Hose of Life from a man's boxers to keep civilization yearning, growing and breathing.

With all that in mind, why did I have a fetish with their panties?

What would Dad think if he ever found out?

I don't know what came over me. I was sitting behind my desk at work, tired as hell, when it dawned on me like the sun that I needed to take a few Tylenol pills. I had a rough night. An obese booty call showed up at my house around 2 a.m. and since she was there and I didn't want her making a blank trip I let her suck my dick. What a bad experience.

First, I took off her stale-smelling panties and put them on my face. I was inhaling her sweet-smelling pussy (a little pissy) while she sucked me up. Everything she ate trailed my shaft, totally pissing me off. A noodle was on my nuts and she had lettuce in her teeth. I shook with anger, but the head game was good. Because I wanted a nut I allowed it to go on. Inhaling those panties, my heart thumped out of my chest when I started to come. I grabbed her cheap-ass weave and fucked her hot mouth. I must have gone too deeply because she farted, and started throwing up on my torso. I was so fucking upset I just sat there, my nut stalled and fucked to oblivion.

"What the fuck, bitch! Those are five hundred dollar sheets."

She sucked her teeth, getting an attitude. "You shouldn't have shoved your King Kong Donkey Kong dick in my mouth like that."

I was jumping out of the bed, puke trailing my legs.

"Get your fat ass out!"

"But."

I snatched her by the weave and ragged her ass to the front door. Opening it, I pushed her fat ass out and slammed it closed. She was bamming on the door.

"I'm naked out here and it's cold! Give me my clothes!"

I was infuriated.

"No, bitch!"

I couldn't sleep at all. I had to wash my sheets on the delicate cycle, talk to my father about the situation (he laughed and talked shit about me for three hours), and then finally, when I dried the sheets, I made up my bed, saw her panties and jacked my dick with them until I came myself to sleep.

Now I was at the office, trying to come to terms with Messy Tessy. The thought of it made me sick to my stomach. Then on top of that Mama has been ringing my phone off the hook. Bad enough I forked over $400 to pay her lights and buy her food because the government cheated her out of some of her stamps. She was supposed to get $178, because she wasn't working, yet she only received a little of a hundred. With that being said, she was also losing her home. That's what she got for leaving a man who loved her to move in with the mailman. But I wouldn't dare say that to her face. Good or bad she was still Mama.

I could understand why she lost it all. With the rising severity of the economy and Cubans raising property taxes, how could she make ends meet? So she lost it all, despite the endless courtroom drama and I had to hold her while she cried herself to sleep in my bed.

I needed to clear my head. So I pulled out fat girl's panties. I smiled at the sight of them, admiring the texture. I had a fetish for panties and I had it bad. I gently rubbed them all over my face, inhaling her scent. Smelled like pussy. I ran my tongue over them and unbuttoned my dress shirt. Standing up, I strolled across the Oriental carpeting and locked the office door. I unbuttoned my pants, kicked off my shoes and still in my black socks I took off my pants and settled on the settee. I sighed, horny as hell. Despite big girl puking on me she did suck a mean dick. I leaned back on the couch and picked up the remote control from the table. Turning on the radio, I smiled, singing along to Jaheim. I closed my eyes and imagined a sexy woman was on her knees servicing my hose. My legs drumming together in anticipation, I lathered my dick with saliva and used the panties to gently stroke my shaft. The texture of the lace incriminating the head of my passion, I shuddered with glee. This felt so goddamn good. I had never jacked off with a fat woman's panties before and the way it felt I had to try this more often.

Clouds seemed to erupt from my mind, sending me into a pleasurable fit. All the things that ever upset me, the way my sister and her troop of demon kids turned my home into Hellsney World, all the bitterness I felt for Mom abandoning me and Dad back in the day, and finding out I had a sister fathered by a man that wasn't my father exploded in me…I was reaching for air as I humped the panties, tightening the grip on my stick and trying to make it virtuous. I loved the feeling. My body felt so good. I wanted to pop an ecstasy pill but I decided against it.

They performed drug screenings at this place and I needed my job.

My body jerked and my eyes opened wide. My legs trembled, my toes digging into the thinning black carpet.

I stared at the drapes when I exploded all over my abs…some of it got in my face and on my lips and I licked them, swallowing my own cum. In fact, I used the panties and wiped it up.

I thought of big girl sucking me up when I ate the cum from her panties. I sniffed them until I smiled with jubilation. I was such a freak.

Picking up the phone, I knew I would never talk to big girl again. After throwing her out my crib I doubt if she would ever forgive me.

The phone rang and she answered.

"I know you're not calling me! I hate you!"

"Come to my office. And wear some rose-colored panties. I wanna eat your pussy all across this office. And bring a friend, too. I want pussy in my face. Tell Rebecca at the front desk to let you in. In fact, I'll let her know now."

"I hate you! But I will be there in twenty minutes."

My suaveness always worked like a charm.

Assembly Line

My name is Trego Eleanor. And I am going to tell you a few things about me. A). I am from Baltimore, Maryland, which is located in central Maryland at the head of the tidal portion of the Patapsco River. As a kid my father, a militant man who used to be a part of the Black Panthers, told me the history of the city. He said if you didn't know the history of something then you shouldn't live around it. When I was 8-years-old, he'd taken me fishing. While we were casting our lines into calm, warm waters, he looked down at me, under a blistering sun, and he told me that Baltimore was the site of the Battle of Baltimore during the War of 1812. After the British burned Washington, D.C., they brutally attacked Baltimore on the evening of September 13, 1814. United States forces from Fort McHenry blessedly defended the city's harbor from the British. A Maryland lawyer by the name of Francis Scott Key was aboard a British ship. He was negotiating the release of an American prisoner by the name of Dr. William Beanes. Key wrote "The Star-Spangled Banner," a poem recounting the attack. Key's poem was set to a 1780 tune by British composer John Stafford Smith, and "The Star-Spangled Banner" became the official National Anthem of the United States in 1931. When he told me this a fish bit the bait on my hook but it got away. I was laughing, looking at Dad and he told me, "If you don't know the history of something it gets away, like that fish."

I wouldn't take his words to heart.

B). I wasn't a very emotional Niggah. I didn't cry during sappy movies and I could give a fuck about a bitch's pussy, babies or feelings. When I was growing up I lived in the 'hood and I was used to watching the slow deterioration of beautiful things. New cars looked decrepit in a few weeks time. Some of the women dressed like whores. Men had baggy jeans and dirty underwear, blaming everybody but themselves for their problems. No matter what business, store or corner house was built…a few rebellious black folks would spray graffiti on the walls—I FUCKED JANE, I'M THE KING OF 20201, HE TAKES IT IN THE ASS FROM AVONDALE TO BALTIMORE, VELMA'S THE 410 SLUT! -- tear it down or let their bad ass children scribble ga-ga-goo-goo all over the floors, walls and furniture and do what they do. In a five-month time span, new buildings looked like they been around for decades. So I did this with my love life. I scribbled ga-ga-goo-goo on a bitch's face when I had to come. I sprayed graffiti on bitches when they didn't do what they were told. Yes, I would get a black spray can and spray WHORE on their upper bodies and spit in their faces to keep them grounded. My women were just that – women and they had to stay in their places of submission. If they wanted a smooth Negro and not a thug Niggah, then I would suggest they write Billy Dee Williams a love letter.

My mama raised me tough. When I didn't do something right she whipped my ass; when I ran home from fights at school she pushed me out the door and locked me outside and I had to fight three, four and five niggahs at the same time. One time, I remember, I said I was cute and she grabbed an extension cord and whipped my ass so badly I couldn't move. She then spray painted

"YOU'RE" on my forehead and "UGLY" on my chest and made me stand in the mirror, crushed and in tears, reciting it. Just looking at the white letters on my black skin did a number on me.

"Men aren't cute," she said, farting. Her fat ass wobbled across the living room, sipping a milk shake through a straw, eyeing an open pack of Twinkies on the cluttered low table. We lived in the heart of a Baltimore project that I'll leave nameless. The lesson she taught me was simple: as a black man I would forever be inferior to myself.

I drank 38 ounces of Old English a day. Drinking the beer reminded me of my father, back when we talked and kicked it and confided in each other. That was, until he was gunned down during a trip to Liberty City (in Miami, Florida) by a group of punks.

C). I have two sons, ages six and seven. I didn't really do anything for them. It wasn't that I was a dead beat dad because I did provide monetary things. But I was scared. I feared raising children. My dad was dead and when he was killed I felt like a failure because I couldn't protect him. I didn't want to do that to my sons – get killed and make them think they couldn't protect me. So I stayed away. My Baby Mama, Kelowna, was a very beautiful woman, even though she destroyed me and I could never quite use my dick the same ever again.

Her pussy curved to my dick but I didn't really think about sex when it came to her. She was 6 feet tall with an apple bottom ass. She didn't dress scantily and I admired her for that.

But let's be real. I wasn't the best looking niggah in the world and I was jealous of her beauty; I was jealous of the attention she got and I took it out on her. I used to slap her around when she didn't do what she was told and if she didn't cook my meals or pay Daddy half her check when she got paid (she was an RN), I whipped her ass with a belt, fucked her, came on her face and rolled over and went to bed. One time she called herself prancing around my crib with a short skirt on and no panties.

I had my boys over, and even though we were watching football on TV, they didn't think I noticed them looking at her ass with hard dicks. I didn't trip. I stood up and called her in the room. She came inside and I slapped her so hard she flipped over the bed. I snatched her blouse off. I heard the fabric ripping in my ears.

I spanked her ass with my boot and took off her skirt. I took a black marker and wrote "You're" on her forehead and "Ugly" across her tits and I kicked her out the room. My boys were in shock, looking at her.

Big James shook his head, his temples twitching. I snatched her by the hair and yanked her to the living room window. "Read what it says on your body."

"You're Ugly."

Mama taught me well.

I would do this up until my sons turned four and five, respectively. I guess she got tired of being slapped around. She started fighting me back, talking down to me and hiding my car keys so I couldn't go anywhere. I saw the pain in her eyes. It was unlike anything I'd ever seen. She didn't care about nothing and no one and she started snorting coke. I used to sell it to her so it didn't surprise me when it became her addiction. I felt badly about it but I didn't show it. I built walls around my heart and I treated her like filth because I hated myself. If my day didn't go good I fucked hers up so hers didn't go well either. If I didn't eat first then nobody ate in my house. Children or not. Mama put herself first and I watched it for years and now the way her inept universe shaped me was shaping my household and my kids.

It was just after my birthday, and I was home alone. My girl was at work, pulling a ten-hour shift and my boys were at my Mom's house. Simmons, Kelowna's youngest brother, one of the most feared gangsters in town, was doing the unthinkable. Behind all that rough and tough shit was a closeted punk and he wanted the meat in my pants. I got off on this because it confused me how they act all street around the fellahs yet behind closed doors they had bigger pussies than a pregnant bitch. Simmons set his Glock on the nightstand and he smiled at me, holding his crotch.

"So what's up?" he asked, rubbing his cock. "I need some weed, but I don't have enough. I didn't flip the birds like I should and I lost a lot of cash. I got a lot of Niggahs mad right now…and I need to get high."

He looked so damn sexy, the softness of his skin foreign against his threads.

Shit, he didn't have to tell me twice. I took off my black shirt and lay down in the bed with my socks and flip-flops. I didn't want to lie down so I sat up, leaning against the cracked headboard.

Simmons crawled over me, giving me some lips. He tasted good. I smelled chicken and candy on his breath. Damn he wanted that weed.

He unzipped my pants and brought out the lumberjack. It was a beanstalk so he climbed that motherfucker until he got to the top. Jack didn't nibble, and Jack wasn't quick and I had to remind him that it was a dick in his hand and not a candlestick.

Simmons was fire. I was smoke. Together we were flames, burning the sheets with lust and tongue kissing each other as if life depended on it. I had never kissed a man before and I found myself loving it. He went back down, lifting my cock and sucking my balls, rolling his tongue across my pubic hair. He kept pulling hair by hair from his teeth and I slapped him in the face with my dick and told him to keep sucking.

"I didn't tell you to stop. Your sister sucked my dick this morning…"

He was twirling that ass, moaning his happiness.

"She rode my dick like a villain. She loved coming on the pole. I never showered. That shit dried up on my dick. And now you taste her pussy."

"Damn, taste good!"

"It does?" I asked, reaching down and gripping his booty.

"Yes!"

"Make it spit, baby. Daddy had a long day…"

Before I could come another dude entered the room. Simmons smiled at him and I lost my erection. He was a street thug, broke as a joke and took what he could get. He got in the bed next to Simmons and he stuck his tongue deep in my ass, pushing my legs back and Simmons started sucking my dick. I was hard instantly. Oh my damn! I had never felt this kind of shit before. Damn ole boy could eat ass.

He was sticking his tongue deeper in my asshole. I felt that shit and Simmons sucked my dick better than his sister.

"Damn, boy. You're making your sister look bad"

He smiled at me, gripping my pole, looking deep into my eyes. "Who do you think taught her?"

"Word?"

"Word."

Simmons looked at ole boy and they shared a secret smile. They started kissing and sucking tongues. Simmons wouldn't stop stroking my dick. Then they started sucking it together, tongue kissing each other across the swollen mushroom head…I was about to come all over myself. They were swapping my pre-cum. Simmons told ole boy to lay next to me on his stomach, and he did and I spread his ass cheeks and Simmons jacked more of my pre-cum from my stick and wiped it on his hole and started eating ole boy out and I wanted to taste some of that ass so I got down there with him and we both ate him out and he was going crazy with huge tears falling down his face. Yearning and burning…wanting, panting and begging. Needing the beef but I made him wait and gave him the finger. The middle. Right up his tight ass.

I felt his hole throbbing on my tongue. Oh, yea. He was coming from his dick and we hadn't even touched him. I loved how the hole opened and closed on my tongue.

I lay back down because I was big daddy. I shuddered under their fingertips. Both of them looked coyly at each other then they attacked my nipples. Simmons on the right. Mr. Street Thug on the left. I was stroking my dick and Simmons was playing with my nuts. I felt incredible. I didn't want the moment to end. I wanted to come and I wanted it now so I strained my torso muscles…telling them to suck it deep, long and fast. Please make it spit. Please make a niggah come!

I sat up and got on my knees. Simmons lay in front of me, his feet towards the headboard. I slowly slid my dick in his mouth upside down, my left foot propped up. Street Thug got behind me and started eating my hole. I was humping lips and tongue, and I could barely stand it.

He tasted my chocolate. I had a serious gas spurt and I farted in ole boy's mouth and he kept eating, tasting and enjoying. When you had good dick you got what you wanted.

Simmons had dreadlocks and the dreamiest eyes known to man. I couldn't lie. I got with his sister because I wanted to get closer to him. We were very good friends but I kept those feelings at bay. I wasn't a gay ass Niggah.

I looked to the side, and grabbed my cigarettes, still humping his mouth and taking Street Thug's tongue. I extracted one, picking up my lighter. I lit my cig and hungrily pulled on it, blowing smoke in his and Simmons' faces. I saw my girl's vibrator by a picture of her mama. I grabbed it, realizing dried white stuff was on it. It smelled like good pussy, which told me she didn't clean it. I sat up, pushing Simmons on the floor. I grabbed his boy and threw him out the bed. I loved aggressive niggahs. I stood up, my dick swinging, my pants and boxers half on my ass. They were humping each other, fingering each other's holes and kissing, begging and wanting. I had to piss so I grabbed my dick and pissed all over them. They wallowed in it, Street Thug leaning forward and taking some in his mouth then turning to kiss Simmons with all that Old English I drank – I was losing my mind.

Simmons looked up at me like a wanted poster. I was the milk carton and I was about to make that ass fill out a missing person's report.

I got on my knees and turned Simmons over. Street Thug tried to kiss me and I slapped him in the face.

"I don't kiss piss," I told him and I meant it.

I saw a pair of my girl's panties under the bed. I took them and snatched off Street Thug's under briefs.

I slapped his ass with the huge vibrator.

"Put them on, bitch."

Street Thug didn't waste any time. His ass looked so appealing. I had to taste it. I was slapping and grabbing his cheeks, putting the tip of the vibrator on his tight, warm hole. Simmons spread his ass over me and I got to work bringing him pleasure

"It's too big…" said Street Thug.

"Shut up and take this toy…"

I pushed it in as deep as it would go, his hole swallowing every inch. I trailed a long line of spit all around it to make for easy entry. Simmons was suckling my nipple…Street Thug was moaning like a little bitch, running from it and I straddled his waist, the panties turning me on and I started grinding the toy deep in his ass. He was slow humping it, his hole sliding against the rubber like an assembly line. I made Simmons lay next to him, on his stomach.

I took his Glock from the nightstand and took out the bullets. I spread that ass and spat in his hole. I was still grinding the dildo inside Street Bitch, I meant Thug. I inserted the tip of the shiny weapon in Simmon's tight center.

He was like, "Whoa, goddamn niggah you're trying to fuck me with my weapon? Damn…that feels good! You know how many lives I took with that weapon?"

"You know how many asses this weapon is about to fuck? Shut up, bitch!"

Grinning, I had two assholes grinding in my face. One on the dildo, the other on the weapon. This was hot. I studied the vibrator. It was double ended. I had an idea, because I needed my dick sucked.

"Get in the doggy style position," I told Simmons and he whimpered, begging for the dick.

Street Thug got in the doggy position behind him, their asses nearly touching. I slowly put one end of the dildo in Simmons' ass, and the other in Street Thug's ass.

"Ohhh shit."

"Oh, yea!"

"Bounce asses, Niggahs! Become dikes on that toy."

I put my dick in Simmons' mouth while he and his friend slapped booty cheeks to booty cheeks with the toy penetrating them both. They were wild and aggressive. I grabbed Simmons dreads and fucked him in the mouth. He was gagging and I didn't care. I wanted my whole dick in his mouth. Since he taught his sister then he could show me what he taught her.

He kept pushing away from the dick and I pulled those dreads like horse reigns and shoved it in deeper and he threw up on my dick and I was done, jumping up and kicking him in the face. Goddamn it I was mad! Just like a niggah. My dick was black and beautiful and the graffiti of his vomit just fucked up paradise. Niggahs couldn't have or appreciate shit.

Street Thug got to his feet and grabbed the Glock. He aimed at me and I kicked the bullets that were on the ground.

"So you're gonna shoot me with a blank Glock?"

I grabbed Simmons and threw his body into Street Thug's.

"Get out my house, now!"

I never saw two men run so fast in my life.

I showered and ignored the ringing phone. I knew it was my girl, wondering was I home. I was smiling. I had her and her brother. I would fuck them both. I would make Simmons move in and be my bitch as well. I would fuck them both.

When I was done showering I turned off the water and didn't bother cleaning up. This was my place. If my girl wanted me to be faithful she had to take care of my shit. I had to take a dump and I was mad because I just got out the shower. Normally, my girl would wipe my ass for me but she wasn't here.

It was around 8 p.m. when she came home. She looked at me on the sofa and didn't saw anything.

"Can't speak?"

She went into the kitchen, setting her purse on the counter. "I gotta cook this food, then I'll speak."

I shook my head and focused on the basketball game.

It was 8:40 p.m. when she came in the room with the plate. On it was a steak, medium rare and a sliced potato. She handed it to me with a kiss. "Where's the beer?" I asked her.

"In the kitchen."

"Go get it."

"No."

I blinked twice. "What?"

"No." She refused to look at me.

"If you don't go get the goddamn…"

"Wait here."

She came back in the room with the Budweiser. She was also holding a pot. "I have your beer and desert."

Angrily, she dumped hot grits on my dick. I was dancing all over the bed, trying to brush it off and it got on my hands and she dumped more grits on my face and I flipped out of the bed, my body on fire!

"You fucked my brother and his friend, you homo! You will never see me or your sons again!"

She grabbed a packed bag, my sons and she left me, moved to another state, didn't tell me her number or address and she put me on child support.

My dick would never be the same.

In fact, I would never forget losing my family because of my selfishness and not being able to do one thing —

Let go of the past.

The Lesbian

I loved my lady. She was a dream – one of those model-looking women with legs that seemed to grow from the earth. She was the type of broad a man said he could never get. But I got her and I didn't want to let her go.

She was a lesbian (who liked to eat pussy more than I do) and she was involved with me. She felt that I wanted her to close off that part of her life to be with me. In fact, I would never be so heartless because I would never change for anyone else. I didn't know all the factors of her life and I didn't want to pry. I figured she'd tell me when she was ready for me to know. I never forced a woman to talk to me or open up to me. But I always offered my ears to her lips when she was ready to spill the milk or spill the beans, whatever came first.

I knew she was a lesbian before the relationship but she was gorgeous and I just had to have her. I wanted her to be mine so I did what it takes to keep her.

I remember when we met at a friend's party. She had long hair and was dressed so beautifully I had lost my breath. She didn't show an ounce of skin but her curves couldn't be denied.

She told me she was a lesbian and I told her I was too and she smiled.

"No man has ever said that."

"I'm not just any man."

"How do I know that? All of you men tell a woman what she wants to hear in the beginning. You make yourselves out to be saints. You claim you don't smoke, you don't drink, that you're a God-fearing man, that you've been celibate for months and that you go to church every Sunday. Then once a woman goes to bed with you we find out that what you told us were lies."

"I have no reason to lie to you. I don't know you. I could say the same thing about women. You claim your lace fronts are the real deal and that you are a real woman yet you cake make-up on your face, sew in horse hair and can't live without your purses, high heels and Baby Phat."

We then started to date seriously. We were feeling each other. For me, it took a while to thaw out. My heart wasn't an ice box, it was Antarctica – period. Love didn't fuck with me and I didn't fuck with love. I've been burned too many times by Saint Augustine Broads who thought Bible Study was held on their clits. I didn't want to take her around my family because I didn't know her like that and just because she was fine and had her own shit didn't mean that's instant access into my personal life. Just because she opened up to me doesn't mean I have to open up to her. There was a time for confessions; until then I'll listen to Usher's CD.

The second reason why I didn't take her around family was because my Uncle was gay…he'd tell her all my business. My mother was senile, but when a woman came into my life she suddenly remembered all the mishaps of my life and she'd narrate my fuck-ups with the photo album out showing her my less-than-flattering baby pictures when I had the overbite and three chins.

My only brother, Daniel, was a womanizer. He'd try to fuck her the minute she walked through the door. I wouldn't trust a Barbie doll around that freak. I knew he was fucked up the day I walked in on him masturbating to a Rainbow Bright cartoon back in the day. I was so appalled I threw cold water on the pervert and told him to get some help. He got some help all right. He fucked one of my girlfriend's to an old episode of the *Thunder Cats.* That was the last day we had a relationship as brothers. As brothers there were just some things you should never do.

I sat her down and told her little things about me. Sex, love and betrayal were the themes. I told her about my foolish Gentleman Years…when I did everything by the book and found out the cover and credits didn't match the page material. Men were egotistical and selfish. They were all for self-gratification, she told me. And I agreed.

"I'm like that now," I said over shrimp pasta we cooked together at my crib, a little after Dr. Martin Luther King's birthday. "Self-gratification. When I was nineteen, twenty and twenty-one, I was put through the ringer dealing with women. I opened doors for them (like Mama taught me) pulled out their chairs and fixed their cars, whatever. They used me for those reasons. Resources."

"Those are good qualities to have," she said, looking resplendent in a red dress with pick tail braids making her look five years younger.

"Tell me about it. I used to have those qualities bad. And they still went out with Captain Dick the Thug who whipped their asses and made them hold their dope. I grew cold then. I then gave it to God, even prayed about it. Yet the minute I went to church older women kept trying to take me to bed instead of reading the Word. So I dropped out of church."

"You shouldn't have left church. Don't blame God for other people's mistakes."

"Deciding to fuck me in the house of the Lord isn't a mistake. It's distorted thinking."

"You sound like my shrink."

I stared at her. "Shrink."*I hope she's not a whack job!*

"Yes. When I was thirteen I was kidnapped by my father. When he divorced Mom he lost custody of me and decided to take the law into his own hands. I loved Daddy but I didn't want to live without Mama. When I didn't decide to stay with him he tried to stab me to death, saying women are whores. It hurt to hear my own father call me out my name, especially when I wasn't yet sexually active."

"That's crazy."

"I feel you about love though. I do. But there are some good people out there waiting to love you."

"That may be true. But the hurt in my heart keeps me in the clouds. Now as a 31-year-old I don't feed into male generalizations. I don't want any strings in my life and I hate puppets. So women can do what they do and I will do what I do, keeping my feelings under lock and key," I went on, sipping some wine.

I could tell by the look on her face she didn't approve of what I was saying but this wasn't about her it was about me. If I was going to change I had to want to change, couldn't nobody make me do shit I didn't want to do.

"I won't be made a fool of again. It's like the old saying goes, 'Birds of a feather flock together.'"

She forked some noodles in her mouth, deep in thought. Maxwell was singing, with his smooth ass. Something about his voice that makes a woman's pussy wet…hitting all those falsettos and shit – shit that I couldn't hit with prayer and a miracle.

"Not all women are bad, but the few bad ones amongst the cherries make them all look bad. So I stay away and focus on my life and my career," he said.

She wiped her mouth with a napkin, extending her hand. I stared at it, remaining immobile.

"What…?"

She gave a heart-warming smile. She was gorgeous.

"Let's dance."

"To Maxwell?"

"Yes, silly."

I slowly stood up, like I was being led to a firing squad. I kept looking at her making sure this wasn't a trick. I hated giving my heart to women and I already felt my heart thawing out. I hated feeling vulnerable and I would never tell her that. Men had their pride and I damn sure had mine. My pride had serious pride, and I wasn't going to let this PYT in on the secret anytime soon.

She gently wrapped her soft arms around me. The feel of her skin on my skin turned me to electricity…and she was water.

"Just move with me."

"OK." I kissed her nose. *Why did I do that, jerk?*

"Life is about motion. You get in or you get left behind. People make bad decisions daily. But you don't give up."

"All this advice coming from a lesbian. What's the story behind that?"

She told me she had a man a few years ago, when she wasn't gay and he dogged her. He treated her so badly she tried to commit suicide. He used to piss on her, rub his shit in her face when she tried to put on make-up. He would invite her friends over and fuck her in front of them. Her friends never defended her because he was fucking them also. They chose good dick over loyalty to a friend. She tried calling the police on him but he unplugged the phone and whipped her ass so badly with the cord that she never thought about calling them again. She told me that there were times she didn't feel important.

She was admitted into a nuthouse and she worked on herself. She opened her heart to treatment and she started to have faith in God. She said the power of prayer changed things and she became a better person. She was released a year-and-a- half later. She even won over the doctors.

That's what struck me about her – her candidness.

Her realness was refreshing.

And now I loved her. I had never fallen so far so fast so quickly. I loved the way she walked and talked. I loved her flaws and all. She smoked and I hated it but at least she worked on stopping. She reduced them from five-a-day to one-a-day and some days she would eat ice cream with me instead. She wouldn't change overnight but at least she made the effort and I was happy with that.

Her favorite color was black and she was close to her parents. I got involved with every aspect of her life and I never tried to change her. But what she told me before we dated drove our relationship.

"Think like a lesbian to keep me happy."

So now I hold my crotch, clad in her panties. I felt so uncomfortable. They were tight, hugging my booty cheeks for dear life. I didn't have on anything else. Who knew my ass was so fulfilled in women's garb? Just as long as she didn't fuck with my asshole we were straight.

Snickering, she smiled at me and said, "Damn, Baby. Your dick is so big in those panties. You're turning me on."

Most men would cringe or even deny wearing them. They wouldn't have put them on but she was a bad bitch and she was mine and I didn't want another man or woman having her. What you wouldn't do another man or woman would, so take care of home first and then go cut the grass.

She walked up to me and released her hair from the bun. It angelically framed her face. She touched my chest and looked me over. Her touch set me on fire. I became smoke. I wanted her to smother my flames with her tongue.

"…Baby your ass is so big. I love ass."

"You do?" I asked, grinning.

No woman has ever made me feel sexy. In fact, I never thought the word sexy and *me* could go so well together.

She kissed my lips and trailed her tongue to my neck. She loved to please me first; she put her heart and soul into it. She walked around me and started to lick my back. Made me quiver. I swore my nuts locked, stocked and fell into the barrels of my dick. Her tongue trailed down to the small of my back. I could have died. I closed my eyes and savored her touch. She took her time, like I was giving singer India Arie a fine piece of crystal. My girl was not her hair and I thank God she had a heart of gold.

She took a marker and wrote LESBIAN in huge letters on my booty cheeks. She spread my cheeks and ate me out and I loved it. This had never been down to me before, and initially I cringed but the feel of her tongue, the way she smacked her lips and rolled her tongue across my warm tightness put me in another world. I didn't let her stick anything in my ass – I wasn't gay – but she loved to suck my hole so I let her. Relationships were about compromise. It drove me crazy. Letting my lady eat me out became my addiction. I got on my hands and knees in the bed and she ate me so good I felt like another woman. I put my face down, clad in boots and she pulled the panties to the side, running her slick tongue all over my right booty cheek, slapping my ass.

"You like that, baby?"

"He'll yea, baby," I said. "Damn, baby this feels good."

"It feels good?"

"Hell yea…"

She held the panties from the hole and she gripped the cheeks and licked around each one. She took my nuts into her mouth, pulled my dick out and pulled it back towards her lips. She sucked my dick from the back. Felt so damn good. I had never done this before with any other woman.

But she liberated me and taught me that sometimes the woman wanted the man to wear the panties.

If I didn't do it another man would and I didn't want her to leave me.

She sat up and asked me to turn over. I smiled at the sight of her amazing tits. She had on my construction worker pants and a hard hat. She looked so good.

I leaned up to her and we embraced, moaning gently and cooing and sighing. We made wishes in our minds and hoped they ran concurrent with our fantasies and desires.

"I love you."

"I love you," I said, something opening up inside me when I heard myself say it.

"You do?"

"Yes."

"Are you sure?" she asked, leaning back.

"Yea, I'm sure."

"I have a confession to make," she said, leaning back on her feet.

I put up my guard. "What is it?"

She handed me a folded piece of paper.

"Read it."

I smiled. It had to be a love note.

"You wrote me a letter?"

"No."

She slowly stood up, taking off my pants. She looked so good naked. She put on her panties and then her dress, barely looking at me.

I opened the note. It wasn't a note at all.

It was a blot.

"If you want to leave then I understand," she said, tears falling down her face.

I lay against the head board, covering my face. Damn. Looking at her you would never guess she had HIV.

"Baby…"

She snapped on me.

"Save it. You don't have to spare my feelings. This is why I remain single. I have a disease and people think it's the end of the world."

"Baby…"

"It was nice while it lasted, Boo. Seriously. To watch you go from a cold-hearted dog to a man of love is to be admired."

I don't know how I feel. I closed my eyes and squeezed them tight, holding my breath. God what do I do? I knew about HIV. I studied it; I was well-educated on it.

But I couldn't stay with her. I didn't want to make love to her for life wearing plastic. At some point a man wanted a wife, a woman that was his that he could admire, love, take care of and fuck and make love to and make a family with and I wanted kids…being with her jeopardized that.

Opening my eyes she had three bags packed. She wore a sweater, and her hair was in a loose bun.

I stood up.

"Don't carry my bags," she said, shuddering like she was cold. "I got them," she went on, giving me the cold shoulder. "I'm all alone in this mess."

"How did you contract HIV?"

"I fell in love with my ex-boyfriend. We decided to get tested together. We did. We were negative. What he didn't tell me was that he had sex with an infected person and when we got tested…it fell into the three-month window period. So when the results came back his body didn't have time to form HIV antibodies in his blood. We shunned the condom and fucked all over the house, unprotected. He gave it to me. And when I found out I was so devastated I tried to commit suicide."

I picked up two of her bags.

"What stopped you?"

"The love I had for myself. I wanted to live. I told myself I would not die from this disease."

"And you're right."

"I have to eat right. I work out, as you know and I talk to God. God pulls me through…"

She looked at the bags in my hands.

"Well this is good-bye."

I started for the door.

"Yes, it is."

"I hate you, man."

"I know."

I set the bags by the dresser, opening the drawers.

"I thought you were a good man."

I opened her bags.

"I am."

"Why are you…?"

She watched me put her clothes back in the dresser.

"What are you…?"

"Open the top night stand," I said, and she walked over and opened it.

"You see my folder…? The manila one?"

"Yes…yes."

She pulled it out. I was putting her clothes back.

"I love you. I don't want you to leave. I have a confession, too."

She opened the folder and saw it. My blot.

"I am infected, too, and I have been for seven years."

She rushed up to me and we embraced. We would defeat this thing together, in love and happy. We would keep each other going and I would promise to give it to God more often because I can't do it alone. I didn't want to be alone, I'm tired of going to bed alone and I know with God's guidance we will be just fine.

We'll do it as lovers.

I asked her to be my wife.

She accepted.

Thank you God!

Choke

My name is Damian Lovels. I was named after my father. I have a different kind of story to tell. And I know some of you probably won't believe me but I swear it's true. In the back of my mind I was trapped in the contours of my spirit. I couldn't see the light and I didn't see a tunnel. I was disappointed in myself. I was a man who stood up against domestic violence, fought for the rights of people and children. I was an advocate for change and unity in the 'Hood. When I graduated from college with a Bachelor's in Business, I built my own company. I traveled around the country feeding starving children and supplying money for aspiring high school graduates in the ghetto who wanted out, who wanted a break and who needed a change. In three years I paid for 178 students to go to college and they all excelled. I felt this was why I was put on God's earth. But there was something that jeopardized all that I was, something that called out for my soul at night and beckoned for my lungs when I smoked weed. The weakness of my flesh had me incarcerated.

My sexual urges were so strong I had to jack my dick and come four times a day and I still went to bed unsatisfied. I still tossed and turned like my soul was on fire. I still searched for lovers on the Internet and found nothing but psycho bitches with attitudes. Women were bitches when it came to dating. They wanted my career, wanted my accomplishments to be theirs and they judged me by my attire. I knew I was doomed when a sexy woman I liked left me because I wore Fila sneakers instead of Gucci. Her name was Assantua Davis and she graduated from Spellman. Her pussy was dismal and she couldn't take dick but she wanted me to take her tongue lashings. When we met she said she wanted a man with goals and a good job. I had goals and a good job. That wasn't enough. She was broke, lived with her mother and was pregnant with a thug's baby. Her "thug" was locked up for life. He robbed four banks and killed three people. I wonder did he wear Fila's when they met. When she dumped me I threw a party at my house and my homeboys, all professional black men with impressive 401Ks, toasted the bitch to Kingdom Come.

If I didn't pay a woman's bills then I had to be the selfish one. Fuck 'em. Pussy was pussy and these days pussy was sold in black, beige, green and blue with lube at the porn store. It was handheld with ribbed vaginal walls and would make a dick spit faster than a bulimic sucking dick just for the taste. On top of that I have an eight-year-old daughter. I didn't bring women around her because she was still suffering the loss of her mother. When I did date I always told women I didn't have children. I didn't want my daughter thinking I gave up on her mother. I wasn't ready to have that talk with her just yet. Was I a bastard for that? One of the worst things you could do to a child was making her think everything was her fault.

My girlfriend, Meagan Pails, Haitian and Dominican, who I used to love and cook for, died in a boating accident with her oldest brother Craig. Neither knew how to swim. Both drowned in Detroit, Michigan. When my father called me and told me I thought he was lying. I checked the calendar and made sure it wasn't April Fool's Day. It was the first week of June. I started breaking things in the house, screaming so loud the neighbor's heard. My entire life turned into a black spot in a matter of seconds. I was fighting anyone who tried to comfort me. This had to be a trick. I was about to ask her to marry me because she completed my sentences and made me feel whole. The night before I told God if he took her I would die inside. My happiness came from her. My homeboys told me I couldn't wrap my life around her. I thought they were jealous. They told me if I looked for my happiness to come from anyone else I would be doomed. I grabbed my dick and told them to suck my ass.

It took me three weeks to tell my child that Mommy was gone to the park in the sky. She had new swings to build and new lives to unlevel with her see-saw. She kept asking for her mother and I kept stalling. I pussyfooted around the issue. When I cooked dinner, normally her mother ate with us. Now there were three place settings and two people at the table. My daughter refused to look at me.

She noticed my dark red eyes. She knew I'd been crying. She knew I was hurting, and she wanted to know why. I felt she was a child; children had no say in my goddamn home. I paid the bills and I was daddy.

After pushing it off, I finally got drunk and told her. It took Hennessy to loosen me up. She reacted the same way I did. She held me and I was too drunk to cry. I showered her face with kisses and let her know it wasn't her fault. I started singing, "Yes, Jesus loves me!" and magically she joined in, sobbing. We cried so hard we fell into a deep sleep. I held her tightly all through the night so she knew her father loved her and would always be there for her and help her get through the tough times.

Between going to therapy with my daughter and nursing my own hurt of losing my first love, I blamed everybody but the Devil. I almost didn't attend the funeral.

Planning the services was nerve-wrecking. She didn't have insurance and I had to pay $5,000 plus taxes to have her buried. My mother wanted her cremated and when she suggested it three days before the memorial I grabbed the Hennessy liquor bottle and threw it at her. I tried to take her whole head off. It shattered on the front door. Mama held her wig, grabbed her purse and ran to her car. The nerve of her! I wouldn't turn the love of my life to ashes and keep her in a fucking Urn on the mantel. Was she serious? How did you tell the love of your life good-bye when she couldn't hear you? Why did she die on me? Why did she leave me alone to raise a daughter on my own?

How did I teach her how to be a lady? How would I show her how to wear heels? How to put on panty hose? How to do her hair? How did I talk to her about boys and men when I was a man trapped in a little boy's body at times? I made mistakes too. I was immature in a lot of ways. Sometimes I would go to a club before I paid my rent on time. Sometimes I slept with women to hide the fact that I wasn't really the man I wanted to be. How did I show my beautiful daughter the right and wrong way to live? Every child needed a mother and father. For months I blamed God and nearly gave up on Him. I dropped out of church and grew pensive within myself. I didn't talk to my parents. I pushed them away. I only talked to my child, building my life around her the way I built it around Meagan. She made me feel safe. We used to hold each other and cry over my dead girlfriend. I got more involved in her schooling, requiring more from my child than her teachers required. We read books on Robert Frost, Langston Hughes, and Martin Luther King. I taught her more about Akhenaton, Nefertiti and Harriet Tubman than I did about Queen Elizabeth. Quite frankly I didn't want to teach my child about Ferdinand the Great when she could be learning about Thutmose and Queen Hatshepsut.

I told my child that we all lose people in life – it was a way of life. That was God's Promise to us – that we will surely die and be judged. This world would surely be destroyed by fire. According to the Bible man would destroy themselves and every time I looked at George W. Bush I knew we were one step closer to the inevitable.

One day I would lose my daughter or she would lose me and just because I was the parent didn't mean I would necessarily die before she did.

With the weakness in my flesh growing stronger and dealing with my girlfriend's death and raising a daughter on my own, my lust for men prevailed. It happened by accident. I got along with my homeboys more than a female. I could curse my boys out and we would be laughing the entire time. Women were different. They had to be nurtured, entertained and spoiled. Females were itching to argue, they always showed a man his flaws and downsized every career goal we had if it didn't fit their needs or fill their bank accounts… yet most chicks I dealt with got weave all sewn in their heads, still spent an hour in front of Koreans getting fake nails with the pretty, pretty pictures and colors and made like they were "real."

What did it for me was when this bad ass chick, Cole, found out I had a daughter. I was picking my child up from school and Cole saw me. She walked over to me and said, "You have a daughter?"

"Yea, I do."

"When we dated you told me you didn't have kids…"

"We're over. I still don't have a child."

My daughter got in the passenger's seat. Cole went ballistic. She opened my door and slapped me over and over in the face, infuriating me. My child was stunned. Her mouth opened. I tried to grab Cole but she bit into my shoulder and scratched me in the face. Men weren't made to hit women but this Ho was disrespecting me in front of my little daughter.

Angrily, my daughter reached over and snatched the bitch by the hair. Her head jerked while her neck cracked.

"DON'T HIT MY DADDY, BITCH!"

My eyes skidded across the rear-view mirror. When I saw all the blood on my face I was infuriated. Impulsively, I punched Cole so hard between the tits she fell on her ass. I closed the door and put the car in "drive." She was kicking at my car. The tires bit into the pavement leaving the psycho behind.

When I went to work I found myself flirting with Tony Dantzle, a new hire. He had just moved to Pittsburg with his younger brother, Jarvis. He was tall, dark-skinned and handsome. He was fresh out of Morehouse College. We hit it off big time, since I was his trainer in Human Relations. I took him out to lunch and we spent four hours kicking it, drinking some Coors Light and basking in the glory of the evolution of the Black Man.

I felt the electricity then, but I ignored it. I figured it was the bad pussy I ate last week, which was why for future references I would watch a woman wash her pussy before I taste it again. Shit gave me pussy, I meant food poisoning.

I never knew I had urges to be with a guy. I certainly didn't feel that when my girl was alive. Maybe because she gave me so much head and pussy I couldn't stop coming from my nose long enough to really search deep within myself and ask myself who am I.

Tony and I always took our lunch breaks together. Women always whistled at him and I got jealous because they rolled their eyes at me. He would smile, speak and focus his attention on me. One particular Monday, we played basketball at the gym. He looked good in sweat and gym shorts. When we went out he tried to pay for the meal but I touched his hand and shook my head. I paid. I wouldn't dare let him pay. We then settled in my car and we talked about college, girls and women in general. He was engaged to be married and I was still saddened over losing my girl. We listened to jazz and smoked some blunts. Over the next hour I was getting light-headed and we laughed at everything. My hand was on his upper thigh and his dick was hard against my fingers. When I realized what was going on I drove him home and didn't say good-bye.

One day we were having lunch at my house and the subject of my girl came up and I broke into tears, apologizing for crying in front of another man. I stood up, wiping my eyes. I fled to the bathroom and turned on the cold water. I splashed water on my face, my heart bitter and black. My soul burned with loneliness. I looked up, grabbing a small hand towel. He was behind me. He grabbed me above the elbow and spun me into his face. I wrapped my arms around him. I felt so vulnerable. I didn't know what to say or do. I didn't know how to raise a daughter. I couldn't do it alone. I would fail. I would have asked Mom but she loved eating rabbits, snakes and deer meat, was a Jehovah's Witness and had some fucked up views of the world and I didn't want my child having those views.

I pulled away from him and he was shedding tears too.

"It's all right to mourn her," he said, wiping the tears from my face.

I shuddered from his touch. I couldn't stop staring at him. We leaned into each other, both selfish and stubborn. We kissed and kissed and tongue kissed and I was rubbing his arms and he had his hands in my pants and I was hard in his grasp and he was loose from my tongue and I was whorish in character and he took off my pants, sinking to his knees. And he took me into his mouth. And it was warm, strong and beautiful. I held the counter, twirling my hips, loving the feel of his lips, appreciating his teasing the head with his teeth (and it actually felt good). Tugging my balls like bags of grocery, I was moaning softly…telling myself it was wrong but it felt so good. Before I knew it I pulled him to his feet. We stared at each other.

"I'm not gay," I said.

"I'm not either. So fuck me now. I wanna make you come. I wanna make you feel beautiful."

I took off his shirt and engulfed his nipples with my lips. My heat traveled to his nuts by Route 69 and his hands molested my shoulders, back and settled on my ass.

I turned him around and pulled out my wallet. I took out a condom and used my teeth to open it. I took out the condom and rolled it down my huge dick. He was lubing his hole, spitting on his hand and massaging it. I slowly slid up in him and he gasped. I gasped from the warmth and the tightness. I had never boned a man and now I wanted my dick so far in him I wanted him screaming.

I wrapped my arms around him and thrust forward, my balls slapping his ass. He groaned, laying his head back on my shoulder. This was wrong, this was wrong. But it felt so good. I spread my legs and released him, grabbing a handful of ass. I spread his cheeks and something snapped in me. Something fell in love with his heat, his body and his voice. He was telling me to take it. Beat it up. Fuck him good. Turn his hole into a tape measure by giving him all the inches. Turn his nipples into centimeters.

After I came I pulled out and snatched off the rubber – cum spurted on his ass cheeks. After it was over I made him get his clothes and leave. I was mean about it, disappointed in myself. Quietly he left. I spent the next hour reading the Bible.

I would never do that again.

Now I was sitting in a jail, twiddling my thumbs. Tears staining my eyes like spilt milk. I didn't know if I was coming or going and quite frankly I wanted to get out of this place. Jail wasn't for anyone. I wouldn't wish this on anyone, not even my worst enemy. I would like to think my parents raised me better than the way I turned out. But I thought I was grown, I thought I knew it all and now I was finding out that Mama and Daddy really did know more about the world than I knew. I was glad my parents had my daughter. I told them to keep my incarceration from her ears. Bad enough she had lost her mother.

I tried to call my father collect. But once I realized that he didn't know I was bisexual, I hung up the phone. Everything was public record and how could I tell him my lover died on me the minute I came on his abs?

I was tossing and turning with him, my co-worker. Tony Dantzle.

I promised God I would never fuck him again and the next week, a week after talking bad about him, a week after nearly getting in a fight with him, a week after I cut him off, my dick was back inside that good ass. I couldn't get enough. I remember lowering my head in shame. He was kissing me, biting my bottom lip. I was knee deep in the ass, feeling his moisture on my face, his vapors on my skin, his slickness on my fingers. His tightness pulsated on my shaft. I didn't want to let go, I didn't want to breathe. He inhaled, I inhaled. He exhaled, I exhaled. He inhaled, I exhaled. He exhaled, I inhaled. He inhaled I held my breath. I exhaled. He stared into my eyes.

"You like it?" he asked. He was madly in love with me.

"I like it." I whispered, enjoying his experience on my inexperienced dick.

"You love it," he said, kissing me the way my dead girl used to kiss me – full of lust and longing.

"Yes, I love it."

"You want it?" he asked.

"I'm getting it."

"Choke me, Niggah," he said…

I fucked him harder, trying to distract him.

Choke him? Nah, I'll pass. I had some big hands and he was about 134 pounds to my 198 pounds. A Rott fucking a French Poodle. Bad enough he wanted me to fuck him while he wore my late girlfriend's panties. I couldn't lie…his ass looked appealing in them.

"No, baby."

So he started chocking himself, while I pushed his legs back. Why this freaky shit turned me on was beside the point. There was something sexy about watching him gag and gasp for air; his eyes wide with surprise took some of the umph from my hard on.

When I had to come he spurted from his dick, and I hadn't even touched him. All over his abs. I felt his hole gripping my dick. I came inside him, like I always did. I lay on top of him but his eyes were still wide.

"Baby," I began, wiping up my seeds.

I wiped it on his tongue, enjoying being a freak. I was free. I loved being free. But I could never tell my parents or anyone.

His eyes were open wide with surprise.

"Go clean yourself up."

His eyes were open wide with surprise.

I rolled over and looked at him. Normally he would smoke a cigarette or finish his blunt. In fact, after we got high tonight we started fucking. There was something thrilling about it.

"Boo…"

His eyes were open wide with surprise.

The hairs standing up on my arms, I realized then he was dead. He had chocked himself to death.

Now I was locked up, charged with murder. I was the laughing stock of the jail system. Word traveled so fast that a homosexual died wearing my late girlfriend's pink panties with my semen in him so fast it made my head spin.

It was on the news. I was clearly embarrassed. Dad said my daughter heard about it in school.

Her friends talked about her. She was suspended when she beat her male classmate with her chair when he called me a murdering faggot. There I was trying to be on the low and his death snatched my ass outta the closet. I looked at my watch, waiting on my lawyer.

I closed my eyes, not knowing what to do. I hurt for me. I hurt for my daughter. I hurt for my late girlfriend turning in her grave. I hurt for Tony's family, who wanted me hung out to dry for killing him. I didn't kill him. He choked himself.

The jail bars opened.

"Your lawyer's here," said the guard and she escorted me up the tier. She mumbled, "Murderer," under her breath. I wanted to slap the bitch but I didn't need the drama.

I had enough problems.

I sat in front of my lawyer, with his anal retentive ass.

He frowned. "Are they treating you good in here?"

"No."

They were. A few of the inmates talked shit about me but it was all good. The ones who talked were crack heads coming off a high.

He looked good in his two-piece suit. The gray in his beard reminded me of his age. With sad, accusing eyes he set his attaché case on the table and looked at me.

"The murder charge will be *dropped*."

The breath left my body.

"What?"

"A little digital camera was seized from your home. Call me crazy but I switched it with a camera I don't use anymore. I made sure I wiped off my fingerprints and disposed of the memory card. I saw your little home movie. On it Tony said, 'Choke me, Niggah,' and he started chocking himself. You will be a free man by late this afternoon."

"Oh my God! I forgot about that! We were filming each other…"

He was disgusted. "When you are released you are to stay away from Janisha."

The blood left my face.

"What? She's my daughter!"

He glared at me, whispering harshly. "You're a faggot, and I don't want you around my granddaughter."

"Dad! You can't…you can't do this. Just because you're my lawyer doesn't mean you can run my fucking life!"

"Watch me do it. And you can't run your own life let alone control your dick. And you better listen real well. I have the digital camera. I haven't shown the judge yet. I haven't told the prosecutor. I will keep your gay ass in here if you don't listen. The murder charge will stick and you will lose your freedom, your life and your daughter. If you tell anybody I got the camera I will deny it and destroy the evidence. You will stay away from your daughter for two years. I have to reverse what she heard about you on the news. You will sign a document giving me and your mother control. You can see her and talk to her for two hours a day with our supervision and for three hours on Saturdays at my house. Sundays she goes to church."

Tears welled in my eyes. I had already lost her mother. Now I was losing the only connection I had with her.

"You can't do this."

Grabbing his attaché case, he stood up.

"I'm gone. Have a nice time in jail. Maybe you can fuck the faggots in here. Or have they raped you yet?"

I got to get out of here. God help me. "OK! I will do what you say…"

He was skeptical.

"You will?"

No! "Yes. Just get me outta here."

"Sign the document."

Reluctantly, I signed it. He didn't even look at it. He opened his attaché case and threw it inside, closing the case. The buttons noisily snapped into place.

"You'll be released soon."

"Dad…"

He looked at me. I saw the betrayal in his eyes. He shook his head.

"I am not your father."

"Dad!"

"I don't have gay ass children you little bitch."

He pivoted on his heels and left the room.

A few weeks later I sat on my sofa, dying inside. I was happy to be free. Ducking the media was intense. They wanted to know how I felt about being caught with a dead man in my bed. They wanted to know if I was going to sue the Department of Corrections for slandering my name. I said, 'No, no and leave me alone'.

I missed my child. I felt like an asshole for what I did to her. I should have never slept with a man, but was that the real problem? No. I was grown. Meagan was dead. I could make my own decisions. I had the right to sleep with whoever I wanted. This was my life. I paid my own bills. I didn't owe society a motherfucking thing.

But how did I get my child back? She had been through enough. I was supposed to be the responsible one. Being in love with a man wasn't a crime in my eyes. I loved him so much, and I have closed myself off to sensation. I closed myself off to mourning his death. I missed him. I missed Meagan. God, Satan was playing a mean trick on me!

This two-hour visitation shit with my daughter was fucked up. I missed reading with her and helping her with her homework. I was her father. I helped give her life.

She called me last night when my parents were sleep and she said she missed me. That they made her do unusual exercises. I asked her what that was. She said they made her draw a male and female stick figure and write "Girls like boys, boys don't like boys!" over and over and I was infuriated.

I told her I loved her and I called another lawyer from the phone book.

It took an hour to locate a good one. His name was Jesse Powell and he said he had won over 300 cases. He specialized in getting children back to their rightful parents. He required a $7,000 retainer and I went into my bank account and got him what he needed.

When I gave him the money it was on and cracking.

He got right to work.

It took a couple weeks to go to court. My father, Mr. Lawyer, didn't understand what was going on. Around 2 p.m., Mom showed up with my child and when my daughter saw me she ran up to me and I hugged her and showered her face with kisses. It was amazing how forgiving children were, yet adults carried grudges.

Judge Brown entered and we all stood. This was a formal hearing. My father still didn't know what was going on. The judge smiled.

"I am going to make this quick. There's no sense in wasting taxpayers' money."

The Judge peered over his reading glasses.

"Mr. Lovels…?"

My father said, "Yes, Your honor."

"Approach the bench…you too, Mr. Lovels, Jr.…Jesse, you can stay where you are. I don't need you at this time."

I looked at my Dad and he looked at me. He rolled his eyes and sucked his teeth. I could see it in his eyes. He hated me. This was cool. I'd rather he hate me for what I was than to love me for what I wasn't.

Dad held up his hand for me to walk before him and I did. The little boy inside me still did what he asked. Maybe it was because I respected him.

We paused at the Judge's desk. He handed my father a contract.

"Your son signed this when he was incarcerated, relinquishing his parental duties. Signing them over to you?"

"Yes," Dad said, smiling in victory.

Judge Brown looked at me. "You signed this?"

I said, "Yes."

"But your name is Damian Lovels, Jr., correct?"

"Yes, Judge."

My Dad looked confused. I was smiling.

"Then why did you sign it Tony Dantzle?"

"Because I didn't want to give my daughter up."

Wide-eyed, my father looked down at the signed contract.

"You tricked me."

"Learn to read before you proceed," I told him.

Judge Brown said, "Mr. Damian Lovels, Jr. You are Janisha's legal guardian. You are free to take her home."

I looked at my father. "Check Mate."

www.ingramcontent.com/pod-product-compliance
Lightning Source LLC
Chambersburg PA
CBHW030824310726
48980CB00006B/626/J

* 9 7 8 0 5 7 8 0 4 5 1 7 7 *